CONTRACT BRIDE

BY

SUSAN FOX

MILLS & BOON®

First published in Great Britain 2003
Large Print edition 2003
Harlequin Mills & Boon Limited,
Eton House, 18-24 Paradise Road,
Richmond, Surrey TW9 1SR

© Susan Fox 2003

ISBN 0 263 17952 4

Set in Times Roman 18 on 20 pt.
16-1103-39360

Printed and bound in Great Britain
by Antony Rowe Ltd, Chippenham, Wiltshire

PROLOGUE

THEY married that morning in front of a judge at the county courthouse. Because the brief ceremony wasn't so much a celebration as it was a legal technicality, their witnesses were a couple of law clerks the judge had called into his chambers at the last moment.

His Honor didn't comment on the somber stillness of the bride and groom, though he took several moments to study and remark upon the handsome infant boy wrapped snugly in a light blanket, who slumbered peacefully in his father's arms.

The judge had heard gossip about the couple before him. The groom had been widowed nearly four months ago when his wife had suddenly died a handful of days after the baby's birth. The bride had been his dead wife's best friend.

No doubt some, when they heard about this, would consider the hasty marriage a small scandal. Maybe it was, but His Honor was inclined to go easy on them. He knew Reece Waverly socially and by reputation. Leah Gray had graduated high school in the area and sometimes taught Sunday School.

The judge could tell at a glance that this was no love match, and that made him hesitate to perform the legalities. Reece's stern face held the haunted traces of a man who'd been poleaxed by tragedy; his bride's face was pale and she had a faintly heartsick look about her. If either of them had consulted him about this ahead of time, he would have strongly advised them against taking such a drastic step so soon.

But since both were legal adults competent to make agreements and bear responsibility for them, he summoned the impartiality of his status as a judicial official and led the couple through the formalities.

CHAPTER ONE.

LEAH WAVERLY entered the den, relieved to see that her husband of eleven months was standing at the patio door instead of working at his desk. With one hand braced on the door frame and the fingers of the other wedged in his front jeans' pocket, Reece stared out broodingly at the lengthening shadows on the patio out back.

She knew he'd heard her nearly silent tread on the carpet because she'd seen the subtle ripple of tension in his wide shoulders. Yes, he'd been tense around her lately, but she'd also caught a hint of restlessness and what could only be dissatisfaction. Had he recovered enough from Rachel's death to take a good long look at what they'd done?

The question had eaten at her for weeks and she could no longer bear her dread of the answer. Better to get it into the open, better to know for sure...

However carefully she worded this, Leah already knew that her husband's response would never be the one she'd hoped for. Reece had buried his heart when he'd buried Rachel, and whatever heart he'd had left, he'd dedicated solely to his young son. There was nothing left for the plain woman he'd so suddenly married, and as the months had stretched on, Leah had become more certain of that by the day.

She knew Reece well enough to be sure he'd never ask for a divorce. Because he wouldn't, it was up to her to offer it. She was certain he'd be relieved, and once she assured him she was willing to work out a peaceful arrangement to share custody of little Bobby, he'd be grateful to be able to get on with his life.

Though she'd known from the beginning this time would come, she'd had the foolish hope that Reece might develop some kind of affection for her. Male/female friendships often deepened into love. Maybe not the intensely passionate kind that he'd shared with Rachel, but certainly the low-key, mutually caring kind.

And yet as time had gone on, Leah had been forced to realize there was simply nothing between them. There'd not been a single word of personal caring, never so much as a passing glance to misinterpret. She was certain now there never would be. She'd finally reached the conclusion that she loved Reece enough to want to see him happy again, even if his happiness would never be with her.

What she regretted with all her heart was that Bobby would grow up being shuttled back and forth between a father and adoptive mother who'd made such a foolish bargain. Though Reece had married her to protect the boy if something should unexpectedly happen to him as it had to Rachel, in hindsight it was obvious to Leah—and probably to Reece by now—that it would have been more prudent to wait.

But a man who'd been devastated by the sudden death of the woman he'd been wildly in love with, trusted more in cruel tragedies that struck out of the blue than he did in the more mundane and temporary events in life, at least for a time.

The fact that Leah had essentially taken advantage of Reece's worries for her own selfish reasons was something she'd probably never forgive herself for. That's why she had to do this for him. She wasn't certain how much longer she could live with him anyway, because the heart-numbing distance between them was already too painful.

When Reece lowered his hand from the door frame and turned, Leah felt again the heavy ache of longing and love she'd secretly been tortured by for years.

Reece Waverly was a big man, over six foot tall with wide shoulders, muscle-thick arms and long, powerful legs. He'd showered before supper, and the clean jeans and white shirt he wore were still crisp. Perpetually somber and taciturn, his tanned, weather-creased skin made him look rugged and harsh. His bluntly masculine face was made even more dramatic by his dark eyes, black eyebrows, and the formidable set of his strong jaw. The thin slash of his lips carried a hint of ruthlessness Leah had never seen evidence of.

And yet the look of him now was worlds different in every way from the man he'd been when Rachel had been alive. He'd been a softer, less intimidating man, more given to smiles and teasing glances. He'd been more open, more apt to speak since he was a well-read, thinking man who enjoyed being sociable. He'd had a sense of humor and a masculine charm that was irresistible.

But Reece had been on top of the world then, completely in love with Rachel, and looking forward to the birth of their first child.

Leah so missed the man Reece had been—the man she'd felt such guilt for loving—almost as much as she missed Rachel.

A fresh wisp of heartache went through her, and she almost lost her nerve. She had to force herself to make a start.

"Is it still convenient for a talk?"

The dark eyes that had regarded her almost blindly for months were suddenly sharp on her face, and she felt the pressure of that sharpness as they examined every soft feature. But then his gaze met hers and she felt the probe of it go so deep that she got the alarming sense that he'd read her thoughts.

And maybe he had, because his somber expression appeared to harden.

''You don't ever need an appointment, Leah. I told you that earlier.''

Leah brought her hands together primly at her waist, not really surprised that they were trembling. ''You did,'' she said gently, ''but you looked deep in thought.''

His gaze narrowed the slightest bit. It was clear that he was alert to something in her face and in the way she held herself. Since she was stiff with tension and couldn't stop the faint tremors of dread that passed through her in waves, it was no wonder he was taking a closer look.

His gruff, ''Go ahead and have a seat,'' was a relief, since she'd feel steadier sitting. Leah chose one of the wing chairs on his side of the room, and noted that he stayed standing where he was, his back to the patio doors and the rapidly darkening twilight.

As always, he kept himself remote from her. As always, she was careful not to trespass. Leah sank down and rested her elbows on the chair arms then laced her fingers together to let them dangle over her lap. She tried to collect her thoughts, but it was supremely hard to do.

Oh God, if she thought there could ever be a chance for Reece to care for her, she wouldn't do this. But the utter deadness between them was proof enough that Reece would never feel anything for her. Leah made herself begin with something mild.

''You haven't given your answer yet about going to Donovan Ranch for the barbecue next Saturday, so I thought I'd tell you that whatever you choose to do, I've decided to go.''

Leah saw a glimmer of something shoot through Reece's gaze, and though wary of it, she managed to keep her voice casual and even.

''I've made arrangements for someone to take care of Bobby. Unless you'd like to have a day and an evening alone with him.''

Leah finished with, ''If you decide to go, we could either use the sitter or take Bobby with us. There'll be other children there, so he'd enjoy that.''

''When did you decide this?'' The near growl in his low voice gave the clear impression of disapproval.

In all these months, Reece had never once questioned her judgment. He'd often asked her about decisions she'd made regarding the boy, but only to inform himself. He'd never remarked at all on decisions she'd made about her personal activities, so this was unusual.

She nervously tightened her fingers and spoke, careful to make her tone practical rather than critical. "When I reminded you about it last week, you didn't seem interested."

A breathless anxiety made a sweeping pass through her insides, and she took another small step toward the subject she meant to open.

"Since you and I aren't…in the habit of doing things together, I didn't think you'd mind if I decided to go. As I said, I've made arrangements for Bobby that you can control however you like, whatever you decide to do about Saturday."

Reece's somber expression had gone stony and Leah felt uneasy. She'd irritated him, but couldn't for the life of her imagine why. Though Reece's temper was legendary, he'd never given a single hint of turning it on her or his son. Informing him that she was going to a neighbor's barbecue seemed too small a thing to provoke him.

And yet the strained silence hung between them and built. It helped a little to keep in mind that Reece was a good man and a fair one, who was as naturally decent as the day was long. She had nothing to fear from a man like him, no matter his temper. She couldn't have agreed to their bargain, much less adored him for years, if she hadn't known those things as absolute facts.

The real danger was that he'd somehow find out how much she loved him, and then either reject her feelings outright, or worse, pity her for having them.

"You haven't got much out of our deal, have you?"

Reece's question was jarringly direct and a signal that he might have guessed the real reason she'd wanted this talk. The growl in his voice had softened, though his stony expression hadn't.

Leah sensed something, perhaps regret, perhaps guilt, but she automatically discounted that impression and considered it nothing more than wishful thinking. A longing heart would always see a banquet in a table crumb. Pride roared up to keep her from revealing even a hint of her true feelings.

"I've gotten exactly what I bargained to get," she told him, then made her stiff lips relax a little into a smile. "And I have Bobby. Being able to love and raise him is more than enough."

Leah tried not to blink at the half-lie in that last part. Though at twenty-four she'd never had more than a hasty kiss on the mouth once by a boy who'd done it to embarrass her, she had the same female longing for affection and intimate tenderness as any other woman, in spite of her inexperience.

"So you're satisfied with the way it's been." Reece's gravelly words were not a question, but a statement.

Leah caught the cynical gleam in his dark eyes and didn't understand it. Or why he'd even think to remark on whether she'd been satisfied or not by the way things between them had gone.

The past eleven months had revolved around the boy, the ranch and the polite day-to-day cooperation between a stay at home wife who cared for a house and child, and a rancher who spent hours a day working outdoors or doing paperwork in the den. The emotional sterility between the two of them had been so heart-numbing that Leah often wondered if they were even friends.

"I'm...satisfied we've both done what we agreed to do." Leah cringed inwardly at the small hesitation, but it was hard to face the relentlessness she suddenly sensed in Reece.

It was even harder to maintain eye contact with the dark eyes that seemed to flicker with perception when she was trying so hard to hide the truth, at least the most dangerous truth: her real feelings.

"I remember we talked about more than just protecting the boy when we started this," he said then.

The reminder completely threw her. She recalled Reece's remarks on that subject with distressing clarity. It had been in this very room at almost the same time of day that he'd made them.

It was the only time either of them had so much as hinted at the possibly of having other children. Or of personal needs, having sex in particular.

"I reckon sex will be part of this deal, since it's a marriage," he'd said, and it hurt to remember the bleak, almost grim look in his eyes, as if he was resigned to the task only because he saw it as a marital obligation.

''Won't be likely for a time,'' he'd gone on, glancing away from her before he'd added, ''but we've both got needs.''

His low voice had trailed off and she'd got the impression that the thought of sex with any woman but Rachel was not only vaguely distasteful to him, but that he also couldn't imagine that sex would ever again be something more than a biological function, perhaps to have more children, but mainly as a physical release.

At least he'd not insulted her obvious lack of desirability by rejecting the possibility of ever having sex with her. And because he'd also let her know that he was willing to have other children with her if she wanted them, he apparently hadn't considered her an unworthy recipient of his seed.

Of course, eleven months had gone by and if Reece had ever had a "need", she'd never known about it. Which only confirmed the idea that Reece felt so little for her that he didn't think of her in terms of sex.

Reece's gruff voice brought her back to the present. "You remember that, don't you?"

His dark gaze shifted downward to flash quickly over her body. So quickly it seemed almost mechanical. As if it was expected that a man who'd brought up the subject of sex might at least make a cursory inspection to familiarize himself with the physical attributes of the woman he'd suggested it to.

Leah felt her cheeks go abnormally hot with a mix of feminine shame and very feminine indignation. Without so much as a single nonaccidental touch between them in all these months, and no hint of personal affection from Reece, sex was the last thing she'd consider. Particularly when the look he'd just given her had been so clearly obligatory. Not even she was so hungry for love that she'd allow herself to be so coldly used.

"I think we've moved past the point where the things we talked about that night might have made sense," she said stiffly, just managing not to give in to the fiery hurt she'd sustained. "I think you've realized that too."

Her heart was pounding so hard that she felt a little dizzy. Her refusal had set off sparks in Reece's dark gaze and she felt a corresponding nettle of resentment. It took so, *so* much to keep her voice even and her words reasonable.

"Neither of us was thinking straight after Rachel died," she told him. "Now that we've had these months to put things into a more moderate perspective, I think we both have doubts about going on together.''

There. She'd got it said and the world hadn't come to an end. The minor softening of Reece's stony expression had vanished, but he was still silent. She tried not to fidget while his dark eyes bore into hers like twin drills.

There was something in the way he stared over at her that compelled her to go on, something that suggested he needed to hear more to be convinced. Leah made a try at doing just that.

''As I said, we made the decision to marry at a time when we weren't quite ourselves,'' she said calmly, careful to keep her tone mild, though she couldn't keep the tremor out of it. ''Lately you've seemed...unhappy. In a different way than before, so I...thought it was time to discuss what might need to change, even though the change that probably seems most sensible is divorce.''

The booming silence that followed was as much a sudden assault on the room as a thunderclap would have been. It had impacted with such power that it was difficult, even in the aftermath, to decide if an actual clap of thunder had sounded around them, or if it had truly been a silent shockwave.

But maybe it had been an actual thunderclap, because the storm was suddenly visible in Reece's harsh face. His dark eyes snapped with angry surprise, and the ruthless line of his mouth now seemed more promise than vague threat.

''Are you asking for a divorce?''

The blunt question wasn't unexpected, but his gravelly tone of voice carried a steeliness that warned how rigidly he controlled himself. Leah felt her heart skip faster, and forced herself to shake her head.

"There's a difference between asking for a divorce and offering one."

The moment the words were out of her mouth she wondered why she'd put it that way. She should have simply answered "yes". The huge tide of hurt and unhappiness that rose up added to her alarm and she mentally scrambled to show none of it.

Oh, God, don't let him see, don't ever let him find out...

"I've made the offer," she said coolly, so relieved that her tone was calm and practical that she blundered into undermining her purpose even more. "What you do with it is up to you."

She'd somehow stood to her feet without being fully aware of it until she felt the back of her knees brush the front of the chair. But whether her body had taken action to help her assert herself or to flee, she didn't know. At least she could see that her more temperate answer to Reece's question had gotten her message across just as clearly as a more definitive one.

Reece's weather-tanned face was like a granite monolith. A ruddy flush she recognized as fury had crept into his lean cheeks, but she knew by his iron silence that he wouldn't inflict it on her.

''I'll look in on Bobby before I go to bed. Goodnight.''

Leah turned and moved around the chair to walk as normally as possible to the door then into the hall. Her knees were rubbery and her legs felt heavy and weak, but she managed to make a dignified exit.

She'd got the job done and except for that part near the end, she'd managed it fairly well. Though she might have delivered it all a bit less stiffly, she'd survived and Reece hadn't guessed anything of her real feelings about either the divorce or him.

The need to spend time with Bobby was overwhelming, so she hurried down the hall to the bedroom end of the large, single-story ranch house. The child's room was next to the master bedroom, and both rooms were linked by a connecting door.

Leah had never shared the master bedroom with Reece, much less shared his bed. He hadn't offered and she'd certainly never asked. Given her pick of bedrooms, she'd chosen the one on the other side of Bobby's. Reece had noted her choice and for her convenience, he'd had another connecting door put in the shared wall between her room and the baby's.

As Leah slipped silently into Bobby's room, the arrangement struck her as even more telling. At first, it had been understandable that she and Reece wouldn't share a room or a bed, and she'd completely agreed. Rachel's death had been too fresh and agonizing for them both, and it was scandalous enough that they'd married so soon after.

But as the months had gone by without so much as a hint of real closeness between them, Leah had reminded herself that she couldn't reasonably expect more. Except for the baby, there was nothing between them but a marriage certificate and the same last name.

Reece had bargained for a woman to help raise his son and he'd wanted to settle a life that had been shattered by death and shock and upheaval. He'd also been determined to prevent his son from ever being raised and exploited by his maternal grandparents, if something should happen to him.

Leah had been a means to get an adoptive mother he trusted for his infant son and to keep his home life in order. He'd meant for Leah to be a fail-safe protection for Bobby if he was no longer around. He apparently hadn't been thinking much about the wife he'd have to live with to get all that. And after what she'd sensed in him these past weeks, he'd surely awakened to the fact that having a wife had created almost as many problems for him as getting one had solved.

Bobby's room was dimly lit, thanks to the ceramic puppy lamp she always left on. The house was so quiet that she could hear the child's soft baby breaths almost from the moment she walked into the room.

She crossed to the baby bed and looked down blurrily into the sweet face of the sleeping child. His dark silky hair lay in charming disarray, and his long, black lashes fanned out thickly on chubby, sleep-flushed cheeks.

Leah put out a hand to tenderly touch his open fingers, marveling at his beauty, her heart breaking with love. She couldn't love this baby more if she'd given birth to him herself. There was nothing she wouldn't do for him. Not even the love she felt for Reece was as powerful as the love she felt for this dark-haired cherub.

Eventually, she eased the light blanket higher on his chest and turned to go to her room. She left the door between her room and his partway open, as always, so she could hear in case he woke up during the night.

As Leah began to get ready for bed a dozen doubts about her talk with Reece began to pick at her sense of accomplishment, but the important thing was that she'd got the subject into the open.

As a successful rancher and businessman, Reece was comfortable making decisions, and he'd learned better than most how to quickly determine and evaluate all the facts of a situation, and then to identify his options. His decision to marry her was probably the only truly bad decision of his adult life. And that had only happened because he'd been blinded by grief over Rachel and worry about his infant son's future.

Deciding to divorce her wouldn't require much thought. For Reece, it wouldn't be a "yes" or "no" answer as much as it would be a "how soon?" one. He'd probably reached his decision before she'd gotten a handful of steps down the hall from the den.

Her obligation had been to put the subject before him and to signal her permission and approval. He'd probably confirm his decision to divorce her first thing in the morning at breakfast. After that, the only wrangling there'd ever be between them— over Bobby—would begin.

And even that was nothing to lie awake and fret about. Leah had been the baby's main caregiver, and she'd naturally be responsible for the majority of his care, at least while he was so young. The rest they could work out as Bobby got older.

She had no fear that Reece would somehow banish her from Bobby's life, particularly since part of protecting Bobby had meant that Leah had had to adopt him. She had as many parental rights as Reece did, and since they were both mindful of Bobby's best interests, they would both play major parts in the boy's life whether they stayed married or not.

As she lay in the dark, her sense of accomplishment and relief slowly gave way to a heavy heart. What she'd done tonight had virtually sealed the death of her fondest, most impossible dream. Though it had taken a secretly agonizing eleven months to finally kill it, what she'd done by offering Reece a divorce was to acknowledge that the dream of openly loving him and being loved by him was well and truly lost.

And it was only right that she would never see that dream fulfilled. She'd fallen in love with Reece years ago, long before he'd ever dated her best friend, but she hadn't been able to stop loving him, not even when he'd married Rachel. She'd suffered tremendous guilt over that, but never enough to overcome her feelings.

Then she'd compounded the wrong of being in love with a married man by grabbing the chance to marry him after he'd been widowed, at perhaps the only time in his life that he'd ever been vulnerable. The guilt and heartache she'd suffered and might continue to suffer over her selfish feelings for her best friend's husband, were fitting punishments that she accepted.

At least Rachel had never suspected. Hopefully Reece would never find out, either.

Leah turned onto her side and stared into the dark for a long time. She must have dropped off to sleep sometime before it got too late, because she never heard Reece's bootsteps as she usually did when he passed her room on the way to his own.

CHAPTER TWO

REECE'S first impulse had been to go after Leah and drag her back to the den to have it out. His second had been to walk over to the liquor cabinet and pour himself a double Scotch. Once he'd done the latter, he tossed it back like a man on fire trying to douse the flames.

But the conflagration of anger and surprise and guilt wasn't so easily put out. The hell of it was, he was overdue to have his meek wife stand up to him. Though she'd used softly polite, tactful words, she'd nonetheless given him a sound thrashing and called him to account.

Leah Gray Waverly had turned out to be the perfect mother, calm and competent, as loving as she was gently patient and wise with the boy. She made certain Bobby saw him in the morning before he left the house, she timed the baby's schedule to his to maximize their time together, and she arranged nightly for him to spend time alone with his son.

She'd also been the ideal wife. After his housekeeper had retired just after their sudden marriage, Leah had cooked his meals, washed his clothes, and single-handedly kept his large, six-bedroom house virtually dust free in the middle of a ranch headquarters where dust hung in the air around the clock. In between all that, she ran his errands, took his phone calls when he was out, and generally made his home life an aggravation-free island of pleasantness and serenity.

But whatever he'd thought about Leah's quiet temperament, what she'd done just now reminded him that the lady had a backbone. Tonight she'd shown a steely pride that was no less formidable than his own.

As Reece poured himself another drink, he did so more thoughtfully this time. He hadn't meant to be so indifferent to her, he hadn't meant to take everything she'd done for him and give her nothing personal in return.

He'd given her his son, the most precious person in his life, but what woman who thought anything of herself would have been content to love and help raise her best friend's child and put up with being an unpaid servant to a husband who, as far as she'd be able to tell, hadn't appreciated any of it?

For weeks his conscience had been dogged by the things he'd neglected with Leah. He'd put her name on his bank accounts, but she'd never spent so much as a dollar of his money on herself. He had yet to take her out to a nice restaurant or a social function. The only time he'd attended church with her had been on the Sunday she'd had Bobby dedicated. Hell, he hadn't even remembered her birthday until four months after it had passed.

After being married to a near hermit for the past eleven months, it was no wonder she'd informed him that she meant to go to the barbecue, with or without him.

Rachel had told him things about Leah that he hadn't thought about for years. About her nomadic childhood, the many abandonments by both her father and mother, her eventual ordeal in a series of foster homes. According to Rachel, Leah's biggest dream had been to someday have a family and a home.

She had a legal son in Bobby and she lived in one of the finest homes in the area. But his preoccupation with Rachel's loss had cheated her out of the complete family she must have wanted and had probably left her feeling like a slave instead of a marriage partner. Hence her solemn little bombshell tonight.

Yet he felt nothing for her aside from gratitude—gratitude and guilt. The turmoil of that had nettled him for weeks, but he couldn't seem to help that gratitude and guilt were the only things Leah stirred in him.

Losing Rachel had left him empty. Any woman who wasn't *her* was merely female. No one to wonder about, and certainly no one to get excited about. His hormones had come back to life, his lust still fired over the usual sights and thoughts, he still had powerful male urges that craved satisfaction, but the mysterious allure of tenderness and sweet feelings were gone as completely as Rachel.

In his mind and heart, love and sex were associated exclusively with luxurious red hair, freckle-flecked satin skin and exotic emerald eyes that sparkled with passion and a zest for life.

Suddenly the memories were white hot, and he relived the phantom feeling of Rachel's lush body pressed against his. His palms ached to slide over her soft skin to tenderly cup and caress, and his fingers tingled with the unforgettable sensation of what it had felt like to lavish pleasure on her.

Pain and bitterness welled up at the torment, and Reece forced the powerful memories to stop. He determinedly fixed his thoughts on the living woman—*the wife*—he was obligated to crave.

But desire didn't rise very high over long sable hair that was usually pinned up or worn in a French braid; it didn't crave the touch and warm feel of lightly tanned almost dusky skin. Eyes that were a deep, quiet blue didn't suggest anything more enticing or arousing for him than somber mysteries and unhappiness, and his heart was already weighted down by those.

Try as he might, he couldn't picture Leah's pretty eyes going slumberous with lust, and he couldn't imagine her losing her very rigid self-control to clutch at him in the high heat of sexual intimacy. It was as unthinkable of Leah as it would have been of an elderly maiden aunt.

The harsh bite of guilt he felt for the unfair comparison made him finish the second Scotch in another punishing rush.

He didn't want Bobby to be hurt, and divorce would do a masterful job of hurting the boy. Surely his lack of sexual interest in Leah was a remnant of Rachel's loss. That and the fact that he'd barely paid attention to her as a potential lover, and he'd never been curious enough to find out what she might really be like when she wasn't being a mommy or teaching Sunday School.

Rachel and Leah had been closer than sisters. So close that he knew Rachel wouldn't think much of him for cheating Leah out of a loving home. Particularly when Leah had given up her chance of finding a man whose heart could be all hers so she could come to the aid of her best friend's husband and infant son.

Feeling gut sick over what Leah had sacrificed and how poorly he'd repaid her, Reece set the tumbler down with a soft thud then made himself walk over to his desk. He picked up the silver-framed photo of Rachel and turned it to study her face.

The flatness of the image impacted him. He tilted the frame slightly, as if to get a better look at the thickness of it, but the photo paper behind the glass suddenly looked as thin and unsubstantial as any other photograph.

For the first time Reece felt detached from the color image, and his heart grabbed futilely to recapture the sense of connection. It was as if he'd known this achingly beautiful woman a long time ago, too long ago, and something in him flinched with surprise at the feeling of distance. It had only been fifteen months since the wreck, and yet it suddenly felt like another lifetime, one that had belonged to some other Reece Waverly.

In the space of mere moments, the memory of Rachel had gone from white hot and all but tangible to something more like a dimly remembered dream.

Which reminded him of the worst part of these past weeks. Rachel had been fading from his mind. A little here, a little there, he was starting to forget the things he'd been convinced were burned on his heart forever. Except for the soul rocking flashes of sudden memory, the everyday details of how Rachel had moved, how she'd smiled—even how she'd touched and taken care of their son that handful of days—had begin to cloud over until he could only rarely summon them at will.

Would her memory fade completely away? Was he man enough to face the bleakness of that second loss if she did? The loneliness he already felt was brutal.

Reece stood there for several minutes more, wondering if he was drunk, wondering whether these strange feelings and impressions meant anything, but eventually realizing how weary he was. What he did next wasn't so much a decision as it was a necessity.

He didn't want to ever look at a picture of Rachel and feel this disconnected from her. The clarity of the photo was a reminder that the living image in his brain seemed to be growing more fuzzy and indistinct. Better to never see it again than to feel so eerily detached from both the woman and the life they'd had together.

Once he'd switched off the desk lamp, Reece turned and carried the framed picture to the bedroom end of the dark ranch house. He didn't need a light to walk through the big house he'd lived in since birth. He went into the first guest bedroom he came to, and moved across the carpet to the dresser by memory. He fumbled for a drawer catch and opened the drawer just enough to put the picture inside.

It was best to ignore the hollow rattle of the silver frame against the wood bottom of the empty drawer as he pushed it closed. Nevertheless he hesitated, as if he might think of a rational reason to change his mind and put the picture back on his desk. Eventually, he left the drawer closed and walked out of the room and into the hall.

The soft glow of the light Leah always left on in Bobby's room spilled into the hall and drew him, particularly tonight, though it was his usual habit to look in on the child.

Bobby was sleeping peacefully, so he lingered a bit before he backed a step away from the bed then paused to glance toward the partially open door between the baby's room and Leah's. It was too dark in her room to see more than a wedge of carpet, though from this angle he hadn't expected to be able to actually catch a glimpse of her.

The mental picture of what she might look like asleep and his quick curiosity about what she wore to bed came so suddenly that he felt a new kind of jolt. He'd never had a single thought about Leah's preferences or private habits, so this was a new thing.

But then again, he'd either had just enough booze to inspire a faint spark of curiosity about Leah because he'd been trying to summon some kind of desire for her, or he was drunk enough to have lost a few inhibitions so that the idea of sex without love wasn't such an empty one.

Either way, he couldn't take the small spark seriously. It would surely be gone by morning, smothered out by the cold reality of another day.

Reece heard Leah's soft laugh just before he reached the kitchen that next morning.

''No, no, let's not put the toast in your cup. It goes in your mouth, silly boy.''

Leah was never late putting a hot breakfast on the table. She might have been up half the night with Bobby or had to deal with the boy waking up earlier than normal, but somehow she handled every complication so competently that Reece could have set his watch by her.

Bobby had awakened early, probably with his usual soaked diaper that required a quick bath, but when Reece stepped into the kitchen his son was clean and dressed and sitting in his high chair with a bib on. He was gnawing on a piece of toast as Leah finished putting food on the table.

Reece felt a nettle of guilt and an equally sharp nettle of resentment. He already owed Leah more than he could repay, yet she just went on being perfect. Relentlessly perfect. Her perfection was a silent indictment of his notable lack of perfection where being a husband was concerned. The mild headache he'd woke up with began to pound.

''Daddeee!''

Bobby's excitement to see him gave Reece a rush of pleasure and love that somehow soothed the rawness he felt.

The baby had his dark coloring, though Bobby's features, particularly his green eyes and the way he set his mouth, fairly shouted testimony that he was Rachel's son. The tender pride Reece felt in the boy might have added to the volatile churn of emotion that was still riding him from last night, but his relief to not only see but also identify the ways Bobby resembled his late mother slowed some of the churn.

Reece crossed to where the high chair sat between his place at the head of the table and Leah's to his right. He ruffled Bobby's dark hair before bending to give him a kiss on the forehead.

"Good morning," Leah said quietly.

"Morning."

Reece sat down just after Leah did, then automatically took hold of Bobby's hand as Leah briefly said grace.

Quick and soft, the small prayer was another unintended reminder that Leah was a wonderful mother to his son. No detail of the child's upbringing was being overlooked by her, while Reece himself had failed to provide him with something as elemental and necessary to a happy child-hood as having a daddy and mama who loved each other.

The boy needed to grow up seeing a normal and settled relationship between his parents. How long would it be before he was old enough to note the significance of having a mama and daddy who never touched, who never embraced, and who didn't even sleep in the same bed? His mood going darker, Reece took the meat plate Leah passed to him and silently served himself.

Leah was so tense that she felt awkward and self-conscious. Should she ask Reece what he'd decided or wait for him to tell her? Now that the big moment was almost here, she realized even more sharply how difficult it would be to actually hear that he would take her up on her offer to di-vorce.

Be careful what you ask for. How fitting that of all the things she'd asked for in her life and hadn't gotten, she would actually get the one thing that would hurt the most.

She put Bobby's plate on his tray and gave him his fork. The thought of what a divorce would mean to this happy child made it nearly impossible to look him full in the face.

"Do you have special plans for today?" Reece asked, and Leah felt her nerves jump. She managed to glance his way briefly, but not to actually make eye contact before she focused on filling her own plate.

"I thought I might go to San Antonio to find something new for Saturday. It could wait till tomorrow if you have something you need done today."

"Wouldn't mind ridin' along," he said, his low voice oddly gruff. "What time?"

The information was a surprise, but then Leah realized that Reece might have planned for them to consult with their lawyer as soon as possible. Or rather, he would consult with his lawyer while she found one to represent her.

"I'd planned to leave you a cold lunch and start midmorning, but we could go anytime. Just so I have an hour or so to shop."

At this point, there was no sense in dancing around the subject that had to be dominating his thoughts as strongly as it was hers. And if she had to find a lawyer, she might as well know it now so she could check the Yellow Pages before they set out.

"So you've made your decision?" Leah asked, then made the mistake of taking a bite of fluffy eggs before she realized she probably wouldn't be able to swallow them past the huge lump of dread in her throat.

The charged silence that followed her question increased her self-consciousness. She reached for her coffee cup to try to wash down the eggs.

Reece didn't answer right away, and his silence felt ominous. She set down her coffee cup and glanced at him the tiniest second to find her gaze trapped by the laser intensity of his. As if he'd been waiting for her full attention, he gave her his answer.

"I won't tell my boy that I divorced his mama because I couldn't live up to my end of a commitment. There'll be no divorce."

The growling words were a complete and utter shock. If she hadn't been sitting, her knees would have given out. In the next second she experienced such a stab of panic that it was all she could do to not jump up and flee.

Reece's grim expression was intimidating, and she weathered another wave of panic. The only thing worse than divorce would be for Reece to tough it out and stay married to her. But how long would it be before he regretted—and then bitterly resented—giving up the chance to divorce her early on so he'd be free to find a woman more compatible with his idea of marital satisfaction?

Or would Reece make an effort for a while, but then realize he simply couldn't tolerate going through the motions with a woman he couldn't truly care for? By then, either her hope would be soaring at an all-time high only to be cruelly disappointed, or she'd suffer through all his efforts knowing every moment that it was only because of his iron-willed determination that he stuck it out with her.

Worst of all, how long before Bobby would be old enough to realize his parents didn't love each other? And when he figured out the depth of the personal sacrifice Reece had made for his sake, would he feel gratitude or would he feel guilt? Would he blame Leah for his father's unhappiness? Or would he figure out what Reece seemed oblivious to so far: that Leah had taken advantage of his father at a vulnerable time?

There was literally no way for the three of them to be happy for any length of time, if ever, under any of those circumstances. Because Leah believed so absolutely that Reece would never come to love her, she ignored that possibility altogether. And without even the possibility of love, could there ever be anything certain ahead except a new level of misery for them all?

Leah's gaze shifted from Reece's. She knew she must have telegraphed her distress to Reece when he spoke.

''Wasn't that the answer you wanted to hear?''

Leah dropped her hand to her lap and gripped her napkin. She felt sick suddenly, so any further attempt to eat would be futile. She tried to come up with the right thing to say.

''You're a very good man, Reece. And an honorable one.'' She made herself look over at him so he could see that she meant those words completely. The hard glitter in his dark eyes didn't make it easy to go on. ''I think you'll work very hard to make something of this marriage. I should have expected you to react this way...'' She let her voice trail off the moment she saw the spark of temper as he sensed what she would say next. She went determinedly on.

''But I'm certain once you've truly had time to consider it, you'll see things the other way.'' She gripped her hands together in her lap as she struggled to present a neutral expression. "I won't hold you to anything but shared custody of Bobby when the time comes."

Reece's face went flinty. "Bobby stays on Waverly Ranch, under this roof where he belongs."

It was a declaration of war. Leah knew it and went cold. Though she should have expected this too, it was chilling to hear Reece bluntly state it. Now they'd not only be emotionally and physically aloof from each other, they'd be adversaries, which made the precarious situation between them even more perilous and destined to end badly.

Leah lifted her napkin to the table and calmly eased back her chair to stand. She couldn't keep her composure and stay in the room another moment, but she couldn't allow Reece to get away with his declaration. He'd run over her from here on if she didn't.

"I won't take offense this time, Reece," she managed shakily. She wouldn't remind him of their legal agreement regarding custody of Bobby, but she'd use it if she had to. It was just more prudent to stand up to him without it. This time. "But if you mean to persuade me that this marriage has a chance, declarations like that aren't very convincing."

Leah maintained eye contact with him, though his dark gaze was fiery now. She eased to the side to push her chair closer to the table.

"You didn't finish your food," he growled, and she got the impression that he might have preferred to simply order her to sit down, but was wary of how she'd take that. It was a relief to have fresh proof that he wouldn't bully or boss her, no matter how angry he was.

"I probably nibbled too much while I was cooking and spoiled my appetite," she said quietly. The gleam of perception in his gaze told her he knew she'd stretched the truth to avoid officially pinning the blame for her sudden loss of appetite on him. ''Could you look after Bobby while I take care of some laundry?''

Reece's gruff, ''Sure thing,'' was a thin cover for his displeasure and frustration, and they both knew that too.

Leah calmly crossed the kitchen to the short hall to the laundry room though her knees were shaking. Had she just made things worse or better?

The truth was, she no longer knew what to think. She certainly didn't know much about the Reece Waverly she'd actually married. Whatever she'd known about him before, mostly by observation then later from Rachel, didn't seem to quite fit the man she had to deal with now.

At least she'd set some sort of limit and had drawn a line on the kind of verbal exchanges she wanted to avoid, and Reece had essentially backed down. But for a man as naturally dominant as he was, how long would that last?

Rachel had never thought twice about standing up to Reece, and she'd done it as confidently as she'd done everything else in her life. Rachel had tamed a lot of Reece's bluster and his natural tendency to autocratically run everything. But he would have expected that from Rachel. It would have seemed odd to him if Rachel hadn't stood up to him.

But Leah wasn't the woman he'd been so fervently in love with—was *still* in love with—so she had to watch her step. She was very aware that she'd have to depend completely on Reece's sense of fairness as well as her own ability to tactfully and consistently hold her own, because it was imperative that Reece respect her.

She couldn't afford to go to war with him, not when Bobby would be the one who'd suffer most. And though Reece couldn't love her, the last thing she wanted was to somehow make him loathe her. It was hard enough to weather his indifference.

And it was more crucial than ever that Reece never guessed what she felt for him. Until now her feelings had been easy enough to conceal, because a man who barely paid attention missed a lot of things.

Reece would be paying attention now. To everything. He'd be looking for ways to keep their marriage together, at least for a while, and it would be natural for him to exploit any advantage.

Since his greatest advantage would be to discover how much she loved him, she'd have to take special care to keep him from somehow figuring it out.

CHAPTER THREE

WHO the hell was Leah Waverly?

His curiosity last night about what she wore to bed mocked him now. The soft-spoken, compliant woman who'd lived with him all these months had somehow turned prickly and assertive practically overnight.

He'd married her because of her devotion to Rachel and to Bobby, and because he knew she'd fight any claim Rachel's parents might make on the boy if something happened to him. She'd always been meek about her own interests, but the child was another matter.

He'd seen the panic in her eyes and heard the faint tremor in her voice, but the lady had managed to look him straight in

the eye and deliver her veiled little ulti-
matums. Though she'd used mild words,
there was an inflexibility behind them that
warned she'd meant what she'd said, however difficult it was for her to speak up for
herself.

It was also a fresh reminder that where
the boy was concerned, she was prepared
to fight like a hellcat.

''Daddeee, mo' juice.''

Bobby was leaning his way, twisting in
his high chair as if to somehow put himself
in his daddy's line of sight to get his attention.

Reece felt the mild surprise of realizing
the child might have asked him more than
once. He covered it with an automatic,
''What's the magic word?''

Bobby straightened and reared back
against his chair as he declared an eager,
''Please!''

Reece reached for the pitcher of orange juice and poured a sensible half inch of liquid into the boy's cup, just like Leah always did, before he handed it over. Bobby seized it with both hands and lifted it too suddenly to his mouth. Reece barely managed to grab the spare napkin to catch the overflow of juice as it spurted from both sides of the cup lip.

"Take it slower next time, pard," he said gruffly, hastily adding his own napkin to catch and blot the rivulets that dribbled down on the bib. He patiently took the cup from Bobby's hands and set it aside. "Ready to get down?"

"Yeah, down. Down."

Reece stood, then belatedly reached for the damp washcloth Leah always had on the table to gently wipe away the stickiness from the baby's face and hands. The bib went off next, then the loosening of the chair tray before he lifted Bobby out and set him on the floor.

By the time he turned back to his own breakfast, Reece realized he was no longer hungry either. As Bobby toddled over to the cabinet door where Leah kept a few toys, Reece cleared the table. Though he'd never done that before, it seemed important that he demonstrate some kind of usefulness to his wife.

He finished up a few minutes later, then set the dishwasher controls before he wondered what the hell was taking Leah so long in the laundry room.

Leah had folded a basket of clean towels and washcloths in record time, started a load of Reece's work clothes, then stacked a second basket of Bobby's things on top of the towel basket before she carried them through the house to put away.

She went to Bobby's room first and efficiently put his things where they belonged. She'd just finished when she noticed that the small picture of Rachel that usually sat on the dresser top was gone. A quick glance around confirmed it was nowhere in the room.

After she carried the basket of towels to the linen closet and put them away, she took a moment to hurry into Reece's room to make up the bed. She was just fluffing the pillows when she thought to glance toward the tall chest where a picture of Rachel normally sat.

The fact that it was gone was a confirmation that the absence of the one in Bobby's room wasn't a mistake. She wondered if the one in the den had also been put away. The pictures had been there yesterday, so Reece must have taken them away before he'd gone to bed last night or sometime this morning before he'd come to the kitchen for breakfast. He'd apparently taken the step before he'd told her his decision to stay married, so he'd already begun to act in good faith.

How hard had it been for him to put the photos away? She'd not begrudged the fact that they'd been displayed in the house. Even she had taken comfort from having them around because she'd been so close to Rachel.

The sound of Reece's voice from the doorway startled her.

''There's your missing mama.''

Leah hastily finished smoothing the bedspread before she glanced toward the hall door.

Reece carried Bobby on his wide shoulders and the boy was giggling while he gripped Reece's hair. The contrast between Bobby's gleeful face and Reece's somber one made her realize he'd seen her staring at the spot where Rachel's picture had been.

"Thanks for looking after him," she said. "If you have things you need to do, go ahead."

"I see you noticed the picture."

Leah nodded. "And the one in Bobby's room."

"They're in the dresser in the first bedroom. When you get time you might wrap 'em up to save for Bobby. I'll put them in the attic over the garage later."

"I can take care of it before we leave."

The awkwardness between them then was distinctly uncomfortable, apparently more so for Reece than for her.

"We could use some new pictures," he added, injecting a brisk quality into the words that gave them the hint of an order.

Leah searched his gaze and felt a pang. This was significant somehow, but she wasn't sure if it was a comfort or a worry to hear him talk in terms of ''we'' and of acquiring things for a future together. It was too soon to hope for anything, not when they were still so emotionally distant with each other. No number of small plans could begin to make up for that.

''That might be good,'' she said, careful to sound noncommittal before she changed the subject. ''When would you like to leave for San Antonio?''

''How 'bout we leave in time to get to the mall when it opens?''

''All right.'' Leah was still surprised Reece was going with her, particularly to a mall where he knew she was going to shop for clothes. Rachel had often joked about Reece being allergic to shopping of any kind, and that he'd hated women's shops in particular.

''I think I can take care of the photos and a few other things so we can leave by seven.''

Reece nodded and turned with Bobby still riding high on his shoulders. "I'll keep the boy out from under foot."

Leah watched them go, a little stunned. The overwhelming sense that something between them had changed was unmistakable, but she didn't dare take the impression seriously. Reece was a good man. Of course he'd make a noble attempt at having a real marriage, at least for a while.

Because she knew they'd both feel better later if they could say they'd at least tried, she'd accommodate him, though there were some things she wouldn't allow.

The most important thing to keep in mind was that she couldn't set her hopes on any of this. She couldn't afford to make that mistake.

The long trip to San Antonio was tense and uncomfortable, and it was obvious that they were anything but at ease with each other. Because there seemed to be little more than inane topics of conversation between them from time to time, Leah began to get a headache long before Reece found a parking space near the entrance of the mall.

The well-read man who'd always been able to talk to anyone on any subject apparently couldn't find anything worthwhile to talk about with her. Yes, he'd been largely uncommunicative for months, but he'd also just indicated that morning that he didn't want to divorce. On the other hand, perhaps he was already having second thoughts.

Or, he might have figured he could go on being just as laconic with her as he'd been so far, though she knew for a fact that he'd found plenty of things to talk about with Rachel. That was why she'd left it to Reece to initiate conversation.

It might not be fair to do that, but the last thing she wanted was to be the only one who tried to smooth over the awkwardness between them.

Better for Reece to figure out right away that they'd never have even a minimally satisfying marriage. Eleven months had convinced her it wasn't possible to have that, not without love. Reece needed to understand it too, the sooner the better.

Bobby was thrilled every moment they were in the mall, and he loved touring it all in his stroller. Reece was patient with the child and often stopped so Bobby could get a closer look at the things he seemed interested in. Leah was able to shop for something new without feeling like she was putting Reece through torture.

After she'd paid for her selections, she caught up with them outside the pet shop, where Bobby was chattering excitedly over

the antics of a rowdy pair of golden re-
triever pups in the window.

''D'you think we ought to take him inside?'' Reece asked when she arrived to
stand next to them.

''Are we sure we want him to know he
can go inside?'' she returned with a wry
smile. ''We'll have a hard enough time
getting him away from this window,
but...''

She was distracted because Bobby was
trying to get out of his stroller to reach the
puppies through the glass. She leaned
down a little to put a gentle restraining
hand on the boy to keep him where he was.

''But?''

''But, I love to watch him discover
things,'' she said, then gave up and set
down her shopping bag to lift the boy from
the stroller. ''I've never taken him inside
to see the birds or the fish or any of the
creepy crawly things.'' She turned with

Bobby and glanced up at Reece who obligingly took the boy. "Maybe that's something his daddy can show him."

"You aren't going in?"

"Oh, I'll go in, but you're the one who'll have to figure out how to get him to leave peacefully once he's gotten a good look at everything."

Reece grinned, and Leah's heart jumped with pleasure at the unexpectedness of it.

"Perfect way to get him out of the pet store is to tell him we'll look at toys next," he said.

Though it wasn't safe to do, Leah couldn't help trying to cling to this moment, so she did her best to keep things between them light. "Oh my, Daddy. What will you bribe him with to get him out of the toy store?"

Reece's grin widened and again she felt that magic leap of pleasure as he said,

"You don't think the two of us grown-ups can manage this baby?"

"Let's just say we haven't faced enough challenges with him to feel reasonably confident of that yet."

"Then it'll be an educational experience for all of us."

Leah raised her brows and gave a non-committal smile. "I'll bring the stroller."

They went into the pet shop and Bobby's excitement over the variety of animals was a pure joy to watch. Reece was so good with him, so patient, and they actually spent a significant amount of time in the store while Bobby looked over everything to his heart's content.

Reece finally leaned toward her to growl, "The owner's giving us one of those looks that says we either need to buy something or clear out."

Leah whispered back, "How short-sighted of him. We could be grooming a future customer.'' She sent Reece a sparkling look. ''So to speak.''

It was one of those electric little moments. Completely unexpected, yet as palpable as a touch, a shared moment that somehow cleared some invisible hurdle and landed them both on the same side.

Leah was the first to look away, terrified she'd somehow conjured up the impression because things between them that day so far had otherwise felt uncomfortable. Despite the fact that this could never work, her heart still yearned for a miracle.

They managed to get Bobby out of the store, and it wasn't difficult at all. When he'd started to protest, Reece had simply informed him that it was time to move on. Bobby had settled right down, and he'd seemed happy to be returned to the stroller.

They left the mall for a family restaurant, and after Bobby got a fresh diaper and they'd all washed up, they were seated at a table near a window so Bobby could watch the traffic while they ate.

Things were a bit more relaxed between them, though nothing like those fleeting moments in the pet store. Bobby grew cranky after lunch, so they decided to save the trip to the toy store for another day and drove back to the ranch.

Bobby slept most of the way home, and he was still asleep when Reece carried him into the house and settled him gently in his bed.

A phone call that Reece had to take lasted long enough that Leah got involved in a few chores until she heard Bobby wake up. Reece stayed in the den the rest of the afternoon, and Leah was impatient with herself for feeling disappointed.

Her foolish heart had already, against her will and common sense, taken far too much encouragement from what could just as easily have been a friendly exchange between any two strangers who'd happened to be standing in front of any display in any mall store in the country. Even comparing it to normal husband/wife interactions made it seem even more dismally common and unremarkable.

Frustrated that she still wasn't able to quell the sense of expectation she felt, Leah went to Bobby's room, discovered he was awake, then set about collecting him and an assortment of toys to take to the kitchen. She had a new dessert recipe that might be good to have after supper. Getting back into her normal routine would go a long way toward putting things in perspective.

Supper was again little more than an opportunity to prove that things were still as awkward between them as they had been on the trip to San Antonio. The only real difference was that Reece was generous with his compliments to her about the meal, particularly the rhubarb dessert.

Afterward he'd taken Bobby and disappeared into the den as he normally did between supper and the time Leah gave the baby his bath, so she finished up in the kitchen, then went out into the living room.

Hoyt Donovan had hired a country-and-western band for the dance that would be held the night of his barbecue, so Leah switched on the television then looked for the dance video she'd bought on her last trip to town.

Her lack of romantic experience included the fact that she'd never learned to dance. The only time she'd been asked, the boy had changed his mind on the way to the dance floor in order to dance with another girl. Leah had avoided dances from then on, though she loved to watch dancers in movies.

Because the dance at Hoyt's would be casual, with a lot of ranch hands from ranches in the area, it was possible she'd be asked to dance. There usually weren't enough female dance partners to go around, so it wasn't conceited of her to think someone might want to dance with her, at least once.

So when she'd seen the dance video on a bargain table at the video store last weekend, she'd bought it. It couldn't hurt to use the video to figure out a few of the steps to some of the more common dances, just in case.

A half hour into the video, she heard the doorbell and switched off the tape to go answer the door. Hoyt Donovan stood on the doorstep. As tall as Reece, Hoyt was built just as powerfully. They both had dark coloring, both were rugged looking, but Hoyt had a streak of deviltry and fun that Reece's more somber nature never permitted these days.

Hoyt was also a flirt whose tastes ran to beautiful women. One after another. But despite his numerous, brief romances, Hoyt was one of Leah's favorite people, though she'd never confessed that to anyone but Rachel.

Hoyt whipped off his black Stetson. "Eve'nin', Miz Leah."

"Hello, Hoyt," she said, then stepped back to open the door wider. "Reece is with Bobby in the den. Go on in."

Hoyt walked into the foyer. "Has he decided about Saturday?"

"You'll have to ask him," she replied as she closed the door and turned. Hoyt had upended his Stetson on the foyer table.

"You're still comin', aren't you?" He'd lowered his dark brows in a mock threat against changing her mind.

Leah smiled. "Yes. I'm looking forward to it."

"That's no wonder. You probably married the biggest killjoy in all o' Texas. How the heck do you put up with the grouch?"

It was a fairly frequent comment and question. Though Hoyt always joked about it, Leah knew he disapproved of Reece's reclusiveness. She had no idea if Hoyt disapproved of her or not, or her sudden marriage to Reece, because he'd always been very nice to her.

"I get by," she said with a polite smile.

"Well, whether he comes or not Saturday night, I wanted you to know before the stampede starts, that three of those dances are mine."

"Stampede?"

"Yeah. Stampede. The men are going to run over each other to dance with you. But just remember, I get three. The first one, if I can.''

Leah gave a bemused smile. ''Thank you for the offer, but the only stampede that will happen is when I step on your toes during that first dance. Once they hear you howl, they'll be running in the other direction.''

''Darlin', you could walk on my toes and theirs all night, and there wouldn't be a man among us who wouldn't want to keep dancin'.''

She rolled her eyes at the outrageous prediction. ''We'll see.''

Hoyt's dark gaze grew momentarily serious. ''Yeah, we will. And you'll see I'm right.''

A little embarrassed that Hoyt was so clearly teasing her about something she knew would never be true, Leah found herself confessing, ''I don't even know how to dance.''

Hoyt's expression shifted to comical dismay. "What kinda men do we have around these parts if none of 'em's taught you to dance?"

Before she could give a lighthearted answer to that, Hoyt caught her hand.

"We'll remedy that right now," he vowed as he started out of the foyer into the living room, towing her along. Leah couldn't immediately think of a polite way out of it until she belatedly remembered the video.

"You don't have to bother," she rushed out. "I bought a video."

Hoyt stopped and turned to her. "A video?"

"Yes," she said a little breathlessly. "A dance video. I was watching it just before you got here, so you don't need to—"

The information made him glance around for the TV remote. He located it on the coffee table, then aimed it at the screen and pushed play.

The video began in the middle of a dance instruction for the Cotton-Eyed Joe. Apparently satisfied, he set the remote aside and turned to her. He held out his arms.

''Well, come on. This is one of the fancier dances, but you'll catch on.''

Leah put up a hand and eased back a step. ''That one's too complicated.'' Hoyt shook his head and Leah felt a little desperate suddenly. ''And, there's not enough room in here.''

Hoyt caught her hand and she found herself turned so she was hip to hip with Hoyt with his arm around her.

''There's plenty of room. We'll just walk through the steps on this one, and not worry about keeping up with the beat. Or the video.''

It was a very nice feeling to have Hoyt's strong arm around her and to have her hands in his. He patiently instructed her in every move of the complicated steps until they'd worked their way in a wide circle around the coffee table, sofa and armchairs. The video had moved on to another instruction, but they continued in the circle a second time, a little faster, but she bungled it only marginally less.

Leah finally pulled away, laughing. ''Let's just say there are plenty of other dance steps I should probably learn first. Easier ones, I hope.''

Hoyt had gotten tickled too, and he complied, though he reached for the remote again. Leah thought he'd rewind to another part of the tape, but instead he pushed stop and switched the station to the country music channel. The video for Garth Brooks's latest ballad had just started, and Hoyt set down the remote to turn to her.

''You can't start simpler than this one, darlin'. Come on.''

Leah hesitantly reached for the broad-palmed hand he held out to her. This time, Hoyt pulled her fully into his arms. She'd seen this slow dance lots of times, but she'd never realized just how very personal it was until she was in Hoyt's arms, one hand in his and the other resting on his chest, looking up into his handsome face. Knowing that little more than two inches separated them, if that, made her feel self-conscious.

But oh, the feeling of being held in someone's arms was such a rare, rare delight! Would it feel like this with Reece? Leah tried to ignore the question and focus solely on how nice it felt to be held by Hoyt.

He gently led and softly coached her to follow. It really was such a simple dance that it truly didn't need rehearsing. Leah enjoyed it, more for the novelty of being held in strong arms than because it was a dance so easily mastered.

That's why it was such a surprise when she suddenly felt as if she were doing something wrong. A few more steps only increased that sense of wrongness, so she stopped dancing. Hoyt stopped moving the moment she did.

"Hey there, Leah," he said, his voice so low only she could have heard it. She automatically glanced up. "I think your fool husband's finally comin' this way. A few more steps together oughtta do it."

Before it dawned on her what Hoyt meant by "oughtta do it," he'd got her moving with him again, only this time he'd pulled her closer and bent down so his mouth was almost touching her ear.

''Forgive me, darlin'. I'm on your side.''

Shocked by Hoyt's whispered confession, Leah had only a rushed heartbeat or two to consider the consequences.

CHAPTER FOUR

REECE had dimly heard the country music and the odd noises coming from the living room, but another phone call had prevented him from investigating. By the time he'd hung up, the TV was still on, but the odd noises had stopped. It was about time for Leah to give Bobby his bath anyway, so he decided to share the process tonight in hope of engineering a better sense of partnership between them.

He already felt like a fish on a bicycle. It shocked him to realize how hard it was to find some sense of personal companionship with Leah, and that troubled him. The secret had to be in doing things together, though today he'd felt like he was only going through the motions. If he wanted to make this marriage work for the boy's sake, he had to do better, whether his heart was in it or not.

Bobby briefly protested being taken from his toys, but then he rubbed his eyes and Reece knew that in spite of his long nap today, he was ready for bed. He carried the child on his arm and felt a sweet stroke of tenderness when the little one laid his head trustingly on his shoulder.

There was nothing he wouldn't do for his son, not a thing. Leah was a good-hearted, gentle woman who'd long ago earned a place in his heart because she loved the boy. Surely he could love her the way a man ought to love his wife, if only for the boy's sake.

That was the moment it occurred to him that perhaps Leah felt nothing for him either. He hadn't exactly been at his best these past months, so he couldn't find fault with her for that. It seemed arrogant that he hadn't thought of it before.

The idea only frustrated him more. How did you get a woman to fall for you if you couldn't seem to summon much feeling for her?

The consequences of the hasty marriage they'd made bore down heavily. How had he ever thought there could be a lick of permanence in such an empty-hearted deal? Particularly after the marriage he'd had with Rachel, how could he have considered settling for so much less? At the time he'd been thinking of the baby, but he should have taken at least a little time to think about Leah and himself.

Those questions and their answers did nothing to lift his dark mood or to inspire much confidence in the outcome.

When Reece walked around the corner into the living room, the scene before him gave him a jolt. He came to an abrupt halt as his brain registered the sight.

His wife was dancing in the arms of his oldest and best friend. The best friend who attracted more women than a sane man would have had time to deal with; the best friend who'd never met a lady he couldn't charm. The best friend who was now dancing far too close to his wife.

And his wife seemed amazingly receptive when Hoyt leaned close to whisper in her ear. Leah turned her head slightly as if to catch what he'd said, and her lips must have come little more than a hairbreadth from Hoyt's jaw.

His wife was not only dancing in the arms of his best friend, she had her hand on his chest. Leah had never so much as touched him in any way beyond accidental, yet there she was, dancing in the close embrace of a man who seemed to have no problem at all getting her to do it.

Reece had always been amused by Hoyt's talent with the ladies, but there was nothing even remotely amusing about it now.

The jealousy that suddenly burst up was so fiery that he was taken completely by surprise. On some level, he knew his feelings were unreasonable. Hoyt had danced with Rachel lots of times, and he'd never felt threatened. But the idea that Leah was slipping away from him stirred up every caveman instinct he had. And the fact that she seemed to be enjoying herself with Hoyt in a way she might never with him, just aggravated him more.

Hoyt led Leah in a slow turn that enabled her to catch a glimpse of Reece's face. There was no way to mistake his rigid expression or the glitter of anger in his dark eyes.

Leah's first reaction was guilt, but then pride roared up. Why on earth would Reece be angry? She was simply dancing with another man. Even if he didn't trust her for some wild reason, Hoyt was his oldest and closest friend, and Reece must surely trust him completely. She knew for a fact that Reece had never been given to jealousy with Rachel, so she was both mystified and offended by this.

Not quite twenty-four hours ago she'd told Reece she was going to a barbecue either with him or without him, and he'd not given a single indication of whether he'd go with her or not. But now that he'd walked in on a dance lesson, he was suddenly angry about it. From the look on his face, he must have considered it some form of adultery.

Leah tightened her fingers on Hoyt's hand and hoped he didn't stop dancing. When their next steps turned her so she couldn't see Reece's face, she whispered an urgent, "Could we finish this dance?"

She didn't worry about her telling question. Hoyt was close enough to Reece to know or have guessed about their marriage, and also Hoyt had all but volunteered himself as a coconspirator of some kind just now.

Hoyt's rasped, "Sure thing. Let 'im cut in," made her panic a little.

She hadn't thought to do that. She'd only meant to finish the dance. Though only moments ago it had felt a little wrong to be dancing with Hoyt and enjoying the feel of his arms around her, she couldn't let Reece think that she could be cowed by a disapproving look. Dancing with Hoyt was, after all, harmless. If Reece hadn't shown such unreasonable anger, she might have stopped dancing right away.

But now that Hoyt had put the idea in her mind, she realized that this could either be an unexpected opportunity to remove a bit of the touch-me-not barrier between them, or it was another opportunity to re-inforce it.

What did she truly want? And would it make any real difference between them either way?

It suddenly mattered very much what Reece did. If he let her finish the dance without cutting in or didn't ask to partner her for another, she would be terribly hurt. And yet what would it be like if he cut in now? Would he glower and fume the whole time, or would they relax a bit and be a little more at ease with each other?

The ballad moved on toward the end and time seemed to slow until it felt like hours between each note. Leah's tension coiled tighter until the song finally ended. In the second or so of silence that followed, Leah felt the hollow pain of deep disappointment. A glance at the TV screen showed the end credits and then the VJ gave the intro to the next music video.

Leah pulled back and Hoyt released her. She was afraid to look up into his face for fear she'd see a look of sympathy, though she pasted a smile on her stiff lips.

"Thank you, Hoyt. You're a fine dancer," she said, unable to defeat the excruciating self-consciousness she felt on top of everything else.

And it was acutely embarrassing that Reece had done nothing. He was still standing in the doorway with Bobby, so it was obvious he didn't plan to ask her to dance, even if the next video had been a slow tune.

"My pleasure, Miz Leah," Hoyt said gallantly.

Leah turned toward Reece. "I'll take Bobby for his bath. Unless either of you would like some iced tea before I go?"

Hoyt didn't allow the silence to stretch longer than a couple of edgy heartbeats. ''Nothing for me, thanks. What I stopped by for will only take a minute,'' he said before he called over to the sleepy boy, ''Hey there, Bobby. Those ol' eyelids are lookin' mighty heavy.''

Bobby tried for a smile that looked more cranky than friendly, and his resemblance to Reece was unmistakable, as if father and son were on the same wavelength. Leah walked over to take the baby.

She didn't look into Reece's face as Bobby reached eagerly for her then snuggled into her arms. As always, she and Reece managed the exchange without touching. It was probably for the best to have yet another confirmation that the no-touching barrier between them was still so firmly in place. And because it was, it was no wonder Reece hadn't elected to cut in.

"Well, goodnight to you both," she said hastily, then moved past Reece to carry Bobby toward the bedroom end of the house.

Reece led the way to the foyer and the front door, more irritated with himself than ever. He'd known the moment Leah wouldn't look him in the eye that he'd hurt her feelings. Once he and Hoyt stepped outside the house, Reece caught a hint of what was coming. Hoyt rarely kept his opinions to himself.

"You're as hard-hearted as you are stupid, amigo," Hoyt declared. "It's a wonder that gal hasn't packed your son up and moved to town."

Reece felt the set-down like a punch to the gut. "What the hell do you know about it?"

"Observation and common sense. She's too damned skittish with you. A woman who feels secure and liked—or in this case, *loved*—doesn't act like she does.'' Hoyt elbowed him sharply. ''And a man who treats his woman right wouldn't get jealous in the first place.''

''Who the hell says I'm jealous?''

''I say so. And a jealous man gets jealous because he knows he's done wrong, so he uses jealousy to cover his guilt. That way, it's the woman's fault, not his.''

They'd reached Hoyt's pickup truck as Reece growled, ''You're as full of bull as ever.''

Hoyt suddenly flashed him a grin as he opened the driver's side door. Though this was a touchier subject than they usually tangled over, they both knew each other well enough to hand out the brutal truth. If one or the other took offense, well, it wouldn't be the first time they'd settled things in a more direct, less complicated manner.

"That might be," Hoyt agreed, knowing his lazy tone would rile Reece even more. "But you've never in your life been this big a jackass. You oughta take a smart pill. Better yet, teach your woman to dance after she puts the boy to bed."

Hoyt watched, satisfied as Reece's face darkened with temper.

"I think you've worn out your welcome for one night," Reece grumbled, then opened the truck door wider to hurry Hoyt on his way.

"Reckon so," Hoyt said his grin stretching. "Just one of the burdens of bein' an expert on the fairer sex." As he'd figured, Reece wouldn't let that one pass without a remark.

"How's the expert doin' these days with Eadie Webb?"

The surprise of the question made mincemeat of Hoyt's amusement and his cocky smile fled. "Eadie Webb is none of your business. And she's not my wife."

Now it was Reece's turn to smile, though it was a grim one. "Leah's not your wife either."

Hoyt narrowed his eyes. "Point taken, though it's an awful weak one."

Reece felt the last of his temper deflate. He released the truck door to shove his fingers through his hair in a rare show of weariness.

"Hell," he growled as he looked out over the front drive to the highway. "I don't have the first idea how to keep her. Not a good first idea anyway."

Hoyt dropped a companionable hand on Reece's shoulder. "So tell her that, knothead. Choke back some of that hellacious pride and be honest. Leah Gray is a sweet little gal. Been poorly treated, so she's probably scared to death you're gonna turn her out." Hoyt paused a moment, then added somberly, "And the minute she thinks you might, she'll be gone."

Reece shot his friend a surly look. "What are you, psychic?"

"So she's mentioned the D-word, huh? Figures." Hoyt shook his head and gave Reece's shoulder a consoling squeeze. "The last thing she really wants is to be divorced. I'd bet money on that."

He dropped his hand from Reece's shoulder and went serious. "But I wouldn't bet money on what *you* want. You don't love her at all, do you?"

The blunt challenge was another sharp needle to Reece's conscience. "When did I ever say that?"

"When did you ever say you did?"

Reece swore fervently for a moment but Hoyt wasn't intimidated by it. "I'm not sure I could lay next to Leah every night and not fall for her."

Reece glared at him, but admitted nothing. Apparently Hoyt hadn't expected him to because he went on.

"But I figure the two of you haven't so much as stood in the same bedroom in broad daylight yet. Unless it's Bobby's bedroom. That's one of the first things I'd fix, if I were you."

Reece's temper shot back up several degrees. "Well, you aren't me."

"Nope. But if I was, I'd tell her my thoughts, I'd apologize, then I'd turn on the nearest radio and dance with her. Might even kiss her. But tomorrow I'd tell her to move her things into my bedroom. If she didn't, I'd find a way to get her to let me come to her bed." Hoyt grinned. "It's okay to seduce your wife."

"Well hell," Reece groused. "Fancy that. I might have a marriage on the rocks that I haven't really had yet, but I'm lucky enough to have a know-it-all *bachelor* friend to point out my manly shortcomings and give me expert *marriage* advice. All my troubles are solved.''

Hoyt chuckled and gave him a hearty thump on the back. ''Shoot, think nothin' of it, pard. Just remember, you get what you pay for.''

Reece's long missing sense of humor suddenly came back. Hoyt must have seen the glint of its return, because they both laughed. It was Hoyt who wound down first.

''Well, I'd better get down the road and leave you to your wife's tender mercies.'' Hoyt gave Reece another hearty slap on the back, then turned to step up into the pickup. ''But if you don't show up with her Saturday, I'll bring a posse to drag your sorry backside to my place.''

He slammed the truck door to punctuate the warning, then grinned over into his friend's surly face. ''Good luck.''

The big engine rumbled to life and
Reece took a step back as Hoyt hit the gas
and the truck roared off. He turned back
toward the house and for the very first time
in his life, Reece wished for a little of
Hoyt's gift with the ladies. And maybe a
dash of his friend's cocky hubris.

By the time he closed the front door and
moved through the big house turning off
the last of the lights, he reached the bedroom end of the house. The sound of
Bobby's fussing and Leah's soothing voice
was a confirmation that the bath was probably over but she hadn't finished putting
the boy down for sleep yet.

"Oh my, sweet boy," Leah crooned as
Reece stepped through the doorway and
stopped. "You're so, so tired. Help me get
this last snap, then we'll rock-a-bye
baby."

Bobby's response was an out-of-sorts,
"Ooohoo, rock-a-baby-bye, Momma,"

that gave Reece's heart a small pang. It wasn't the first time the child had gotten too tired and then become fussy, but Leah handled it as she always did, with tenderness and unrushed patience.

The small pang became an ache that felt almost like affection. Almost like longing. The crazy yearning to be crooned over and soothed like she was doing with the boy seemed profoundly childish, and yet it uncovered a need for comfort that he'd never admitted, not even to himself.

Reece watched from the doorway as Leah finished with the baby's nightshirt then started to lift him from the bed. Bobby grabbed for her and managed instead to tear one side of her hair from the barrette. Without missing a beat, Leah reached up to pull the barrette free, and her shiny sable hair rippled down to flow past her shoulders then down her back to her narrow waist.

Reece was struck by the elegance of the way it had fallen, and the rich shine as the soft lamplight caught it. It'd been years since he'd seen Leah wear her hair loose, and she'd never worn it this long. Then again, he might have seen her wear it down sometime in the past few months, but it hadn't made much of an impression on him.

It made an impression now, and Reece felt a burst of sensual heat that signaled a reassuring stir of male interest. Leah looked less reserved and aloof with her hair down, less matronly, more…feminine.

Still oblivious to Reece's presence in the doorway, she tossed the barrette in the direction of the dresser, caught a swath of her hair to gently pull it away from Bobby's hand, then picked up the child and the small stuffed pony that was one of Bobby's favorites.

Bobby clung to her neck, crying nearly full-throttle now, but she turned to walk calmly to the rocking chair to sit down. She didn't see Reece until she tried to offer the pony to the fussy boy.

Her gaze dropped back to Bobby as he clutched the pony and then put his head down on her shoulder. Somehow he managed to keep the pony tucked under his arm while he sucked his thumb. Leah started rocking and the fretful howls continued for a few moments, then began to wind down.

Reece crossed the room to crouch down beside the rocking chair and place his hand on the boy's back. Bobby turned his head and focused on him, and quieted even more.

''He feels a little warm tonight,'' Leah remarked quietly, and Reece could tell by the tiny waver in her voice that she was even more uneasy with him than she'd

been before. ''There's an ear infection going around. If he has a bad night or he's
not feeling better in the morning, I'll call
the doctor.''

Bobby's howls were now little more
than babyish gurgles that were more evidence of growing contentment. He blinked
his eyes heavily a time or two as he struggled to keep them open. Leah continued to
rock as Bobby finally went silent and his
eyelids dropped closed a last time.

Reece shifted his hand down the boy's
small back until it hovered a bare inch
from Leah's fingers.

''I was out of line earlier,'' he said,
keeping his voice low. ''Been out of line
for a long time, and I want to apologize.
It's a fact that I don't know what to do
with you or about you, but I didn't mean
to hurt your feelings. Not tonight and not
all the other times I must have. I've been
selfish and I've been thoughtless.''

Leah's blue gaze shifted toward him and he saw clearly her wary surprise, though it was obvious to him that she thought she'd concealed it.

As apologies went, it was stiff and almost sounded rehearsed, but Leah sensed it was genuine. The wonder of that sent such a swell of emotion through her that she felt a sharp sting of tears. The sting brought with it a thick feeling in her throat that panicked her. She couldn't let Reece see how much this meant, and yet it would be churlish not to be gracious. Surely she could do that much without giving anything away.

"I appreciate that you told me. Thank you." Certain that would be the end of it, Leah glanced away.

But the moment Reece's big hand eased down to warmly cover hers, Leah jumped and her gaze flew to his. The small start roused Bobby, who made a noise of protest and lifted his head slightly before he dropped it back down on her shoulder and relaxed again.

The sudden gleam in Reece's gaze told Leah he'd been surprised by her involuntary reaction to his unexpected touch, but then his face went utterly somber.

The warm feeling of his hard, callused hand made her skin tingle. Just one simple touch from Reece affected her more powerfully than being in Hoyt's arms, and somehow that made everything more tragic. It would have been better to never know.

"I reckon I've left off touching you so long that you're bound to jump when I do it now." The gravelly texture of Reece's low voice seemed to invade her because she felt it low in her middle.

Leah almost couldn't defeat the emotion that had risen higher at his small confession. She tried to give him a small smile without actually looking at his face. Her "I'm probably just...tired," came out as choked as it felt. To cover it, she said a quick, "Would you like to rock him?"

Leah immediately felt guilty for the nervous offer because it would disrupt the baby who'd just settled down. And because she'd offered solely to distract Reece. Her tension shot higher.

"It's my fault you're so uneasy with me that you'd like to run."

Leah's face went hot and she felt painfully transparent. The Reece Waverly of the past several months hadn't been perceptive at all. Even worse, the soft gruffness in his low voice and the way it sent a velvety sensation through her was something she was compelled to resist.

She didn't dare look at him. "As I said, I'm tired. It's been a long day."

Leah's nerves screamed with the tension now. It was a wonder that Bobby hadn't sensed it, but then, judging from the heavy way he laid against her, he was probably long gone.

Her soft, ''Is he asleep?'' managed to give away a hint of the desperation she felt, but she couldn't seem to help that either. Only a determined act of will helped her to slide her hand from beneath Reece's before he could answer. She almost breathed a sigh of relief when his hand fell away.

Irrationally worried that Reece might somehow counter her move away and touch her again, she gently gathered Bobby and stood to carry him to his bed. Reece followed to look on as she carefully laid the boy on his back. Leah spared a moment to move her hair out of the way before she set the stuffed pony aside.

Reece had gripped the bed rail, so she drew the light blanket up to cover the boy to his chest before she stepped back. Reece silently lifted the side of the bed into place until the catch snapped securely.

Leah was about to turn away when Reece caught her elbow. His hard fingers were gentle, but she felt the steely inflexibility in them. The contrast between Reece's towering height and hard male physique and her own much smaller stature and feminine softness had never impacted her as strongly as in that moment.

Reece was literally big enough to force her to do anything he wanted, yet despite the steel in his gentle grip she was aware every second that all it would take was one word or one move on her part to get him to release her. The impression was powerful.

More powerful still was the near paralysis she felt as sensation after sensation whirled and spiraled through her just because he'd caught her arm and was standing so close. An expectation she'd never felt this acutely in her whole life began to glitter and rise.

What would happen now? What would Reece do?

Or was she making too much of this?

CHAPTER FIVE

"I DON'T remember your hair being so long," Reece said gruffly, and Leah felt something like a fist close around her heart to lightly squeeze.

Reece turned her more fully toward him and lifted his free hand.

"I see some stray hairpins," he remarked, his voice going smoky now.

Leah actually quivered when his big fingers plucked gently at her hair. Her knees went weak at the delicate sensations that poured over her scalp and streamed down her body.

The utter magic of Reece's gentle search could overcome her reserve in mere seconds and she had to stop him while she still had the will to try. Leah jerked up a hand to feel for the pins.

"Wh-why don't you check Bobby's bed for others?" she said shakily, somehow managing to turn away and pull her elbow from Reece's grip at the same time. "I always use a certain number, so I'll know if any are lost," she babbled on. "Bobby might put them in his mouth, you know."

Reece caught her hand and she was instantly immobilized.

"So we'll count the ones you have left," he said, as he turned her to face him again. Leah's body ignored the protest of her panicked brain. "No sense disturbing the boy with a search till we know."

The sensation of Reece lightly touching and plucking and sometimes running his fingers through her hair made Leah so breathless that she felt dizzy. She'd never imagined anyone's touch could have this effect on her, not even Reece's.

But he had so much more experience than she did, he knew so much more. Her deep, deep craving to touch and be touched, to love and be loved, made her as vulnerable to this—to Reece—as her inexperience did.

"You have beautiful hair," he rasped, and she felt the warm puffs of his breath feather lightly across the crown of her head. "I never knew it would be this soft."

Leah was completely paralyzed by what he was doing to her, and she stared at his chest in a near hypnotic daze as Reece slipped her hairpins into his shirt pocket. Her eyelids dropped shut helplessly on the sight, and when Reece's big fingers combed lightly into the hair at the sides of her face, she felt like she was sinking into a sweet ocean of sensation.

Reece gently gripped her head to tilt it back, and she didn't have the power to lift her hands to steady herself much less stop him. Leah was dimly aware that she tried to speak, and she must have because she heard herself say the words.

"Don't...please."

"How are you gonna stop me?"

The low question was so muted that it felt as if it had been spoken in a distant room. The magic that radiated through her from Reece's warm hands zoomed low to impact her most feminine places, and she couldn't think of an effective way to answer him. She wasn't sure she wanted to.

The cool touch of his firm mouth on her slightly open lips made her draw in a quick breath. Reece toyed lazily with her lips, then pressed a little more firmly.

Leah felt a feeble stir of self-consciousness, but it evaporated in a heart-beat as Reece's mouth became a little more aggressive. She felt her palms cover the backs of Reece's big hands, but she was only barely conscious of the fact that she'd been able to lift them after all. She was shaking all over but still the nibbling, teasing and periodic demand of his lips went on.

Her insides had melted and now bubbled with a wild heat that demonstrated to her just how complete her prior ignorance of intimate things had been. And how helpless she was to control her reaction to this first introduction.

If Reece's lips hadn't eased away from hers that moment, she might truly have fainted. As it was, she clung weakly to his thick wrists. He lowered his hands to her waist and gripped it firmly. Her hands settled naturally on his hard chest. Her palms felt scorched by the heat of him through the taut cotton of his shirt, and she felt the echo of her own pounding heartbeat beneath her fingers.

As the universe slowly came back into focus, Leah began to feel ashamed of the way she'd responded to Reece. She'd heard about ''knee-weakening'' kisses, but she'd not taken the idea seriously. And since at twenty-four this had been the first true kiss of her life, she was even more embarrassed over what had surely been an unsophisticated response.

The worst part was that she knew without looking up at Reece's face that he must have guessed that. And that he'd also realized he'd just stumbled on a sure way to manipulate her.

If he chose to use it against her.

''I—I wish you hadn't...''

The surprise of hearing herself speak was more troubling evidence that she'd somehow lost the ability to think circumspectly before she spoke. But then, her response should have already told Reece everything he needed to know. Or *almost* everything.

''We're done living like roommates,'' he growled and she felt the harsh possessiveness beneath the words. "Tonight's the start. Tomorrow we'll put our things together."

Reece's blunt decree jolted Leah further out of her sensual fog. As if he'd felt her immediate resistance to the idea, he went on.

"I'm not ready for sex either, but we've got a marriage to live up to. Husbands and wives share a bed."

Leah pressed against his chest. Reece loosened his hold to allow her to distance herself, but he caught her hand lightly as she stepped back and prompted her to look up into his face. The moment she did, he released his hold on her fingers.

"You were right about this marriage," he said starkly. "We made it when we shouldn't have, and now we're facing the consequences. But divorce carries its own consequences. Worse ones for Bobby than for us."

Leah felt her resistance weaken at the reminder and she couldn't seem to help that her gaze shifted toward the sleeping boy. Reece's low words brought her attention back to him.

"I won't rush into another mistake, so I mean to give this marriage some effort. Serious effort."

Leah started to glance away evasively when he added, "I reckon you aren't as aloof now as you were."

Male knowledge glittered in his dark eyes. Leah didn't know how to answer him, much less how to credibly deny what he'd said.

However much she'd tried to squelch it, some part of her had still wanted to know what it would be like to be the focus of Reece's romantic attention. Though common sense predicted how very risky and doomed to fail the actual experience would be, after what had happened moments ago,

Reece's near-mandate was not as objectionable as it should have been. In fact, she couldn't seem to summon much objection to it at all.

A feeling of inevitability stole over her. It was already obvious that Reece would never let up until she did what he wanted and tried to save this marriage. And perhaps they should give it serious effort. When they tried and then failed, the foolish hopes that had been stirred up again by that kiss would have long since been pounded out of her heart.

At least she'd never wonder if she could have done something more to spare Bobby the hurt of divorce, though she'd carry that eventual failure with her to the end of her days.

Leah dropped her gaze from Reece's and turned away though she sensed his expectation too strongly to leave the room. It was as if she was tethered to him by some invisible cord.

"Leah?"

The smoky gruffness of his low voice pulled at something in her and she felt her heart break a little. When Reece decided he couldn't be happy with her, she'd be devastated, and yet the obligation she felt to Bobby was keen.

"Tomorrow, Leah. I can help you move your things or I can look after Bobby while you do."

Leah's back was to Reece, so she lifted her hands to press her fingers over her still sensitive lips. She could still feel that long, deliciously long, kiss. She mentally reviewed all her objections, then squeezed her eyes closed as she accepted what lay ahead. She lowered her hands and straightened a bit.

"There's something I want you to do first," she said quietly, then turned to face him. It took an incredible amount of nerve to get the words out, but it was suddenly imperative that she do so. Since Reece was insisting on this, she wanted something in return for agreeing to do what, in essence, was guaranteed to become the most devastating heartbreak of her life.

''I'd like you to switch the bed you've been sleeping in with one of the guest room beds. Or even the one in my room,'' she said, then hesitated when she saw the faint surprise in Reece's dark gaze before she went on.

''I'm not sure I want to explain why I don't want to share that one with you, but I don't. I'd also appreciate any other changes you might...make.''

Specifically, she meant the few things of Rachel's that were still in his room—Rachel's jewelry box on the dresser for one—and in his closet. And, as far as she knew, there might even be something of

Rachel's left in the drawers. Reece had packed up most of her things and either stored them or given them away months ago.

Leah didn't believe either of them needed to have daily reminders of Rachel—not in that bedroom—and when she moved her things into the drawers Rachel had used, she didn't want to happen across anything she'd have to remove. It was better for them both if Reece did that himself.

And it might be prudent for Reece to at least go through one final ritual of removing Rachel's things. It would be a last chance for him to change his mind because it would be a graphic reminder that he was replacing the woman he'd deeply loved with one he might never love.

Though she'd loved Rachel and knew she'd live in her shadow for as long as this marriage lasted, Leah needed to feel as if she had as full an opportunity as possible to make her own small place with Reece, however pessimistic she was about actually being able to do that.

She was married to Rachel's husband and she was raising Rachel's son. Though Leah didn't imagine anything she could ever do or be to Reece would ever eclipse Rachel, she at least wanted something that was "Leah's," even if it was only a bed. Besides which, Leah wasn't certain if she could bring herself to sleep in the bed Reece had shared with Rachel, since it represented the most intimate part of their lives together.

Reece's expression slowly grew solemn as the understanding of what she was asking sunk in.

"I'll take care of it."

The words were brusque, and Leah wondered if he realized how forced they sounded, as if he was making himself agree to do something he loathed.

"Well then," she said stiffly after a moment, "I need to get to bed."

"How many hairpins?" Reece's question stopped her and she gave a quick, "Eight. How many did you find?"

"Eight."

He reached into his shirt pocket to get them out. Leah walked to him and held out her hand. Reece dropped them into her palm, and his fingers lightly brushed her skin. As recently as an hour ago that might not have happened. Leah closed her fingers on the pins.

"Thank you." She couldn't fully make eye contact as she murmured a soft, "Goodnight."

"Night."

Leah turned and walked to Bobby's dresser for her discarded barrette then moved as calmly as she could into the room that would be her sanctuary only one night more. She was relieved beyond words when she was able to close the door and lean back wearily against it.

She'd been afraid Reece would kiss her again, but she'd sensed his upset with her over the bed and Rachel's things, so she shouldn't have worried.

The suddenness of everything tonight sent a fresh shock through her that was followed by a huge wave of fatigue. When she summoned the energy to straighten and cross to her private bathroom, she had to practically drag herself through the motions of undressing and taking her shower.

By the time she'd finished getting ready for bed and opened the door to Bobby's room a few inches, she was too worn out to do anything more than crawl into her bed and fall instantly asleep.

Early that next morning, Reece announced that they were going to San Antonio to shop for new bedroom furniture. Though Leah had protested the unnecessary expense, Reece rejected the notion.

"You can either help me pick it out or suffer my choice," he'd told her, and she felt a little sick that her demand last night had led to this.

"Please, Reece. I don't want to do this. If this is your way to make me back down, then I will. Replacing everything will be an incredible expense, even if we don't match the quality of what you already have. And there are four other beds in this house, so it's a foolish waste of money."

"It's Waverly money," he'd said tersely. "It's about time the Waverlys got some new things around here."

His stern expression seemed to soften fractionally. "You can pick one of the guest bedroom sets to donate to charity and set up my old one in that room. Maybe some family in the church could use the one you pick to give away. It's all good quality.''

The suggestion was a fine one that muted some of her objection. She thought right away of a family who might benefit.

''That's a very generous idea,'' she said, but Reece cut across what she was saying, bluntly ignoring her praise.

''The men'll be here in a half hour to move everything out.''

Leah immediately thought of the things that should be done before they arrived and rushed through her breakfast. She left Bobby in Reece's care while she hurried in to strip the bed and move the lamps and the things on top of the chests and dresser to one of the guest rooms.

The fact that Rachel's jewelry box was missing made her realize Reece must have cleared her things away last night or done it before he'd come out to breakfast. She was touched by his quick action, particularly since she knew it must have been difficult for him.

Leah barely finished her preparations before the ranch hands arrived. She took charge of Bobby while everything was moved out and divided between the three guest bedrooms. The clothing in the drawers could stay where it was until the replacement furniture was delivered. All that was left was for Leah to run the vacuum in the now empty bedroom, which took more time than usual because there was so much more exposed carpet and she also took time to use the edger attachment along the baseboards.

Though Leah was skeptical they could find replacements and have them all delivered that day, Reece seemed confident that it could be done. Nevertheless, they packed up Bobby and left for San Antonio in time to arrive when the furniture store opened.

Leah was appalled at the prices for the fine quality solid wood furniture Reece insisted upon and told him so when the saleswoman stepped out of earshot to check on the availability of a chest they'd been looking at. For the first time that morning, Reece slid his arm around her waist and leaned down.

"We could replace every stick of furniture in the house and not feel the slightest ripple in Waverly net worth." Now his rugged face went more stern. "So if you pick something just because you think it's cheaper, I'll pick the most expensive set in the place and you'll be stuck with it."

Leah squirmed inwardly at the small threat. "If I'd known you'd do this, I wouldn't ha—"

"If you hadn't, I would have. If we'd done this right from the beginning, we would have come here before we made the trip to the courthouse.''

The saleswoman came bustling back, all smiles. She took a moment to say something playful to Bobby who was becoming impatient because the stroller was sitting still, before she told them the chest could be ordered. Because they needed the furniture that day, they moved on to another room setting.

Leah managed to get Reece to make the actual selection, and he picked the impressive four-poster bed with matching pieces that she'd secretly admired. Reece took care of the payment and delivery arrangements while Leah got Bobby a drink of water and a fresh diaper.

Though she'd been skeptical of Reece's ability to have the furniture delivered that day, he'd got it done. A new bedspread and bedding came next, since the window treatment in the master bedroom was a neutral one she liked. Leah selected drawer liners and they took those things with them, along with a tired and hungry little boy who could no longer be put off with crackers.

They had lunch before they left town, then settled Bobby in his car seat for the long ride home. There was a pleasant sense of ease between them. Reece had touched her casually, but often enough to maintain the growing sense of connection between them. Now the long silences between them didn't feel so empty and Leah began to grow more comfortable with them.

They arrived home an hour ahead of the furniture truck and that gave Leah time to launder the new bedding. She kept Bobby out of the way while the furniture was carried into the house. Reece had her direct the placement of the pieces, and she let Bobby watch as the big bed was assembled and the new mattress and box springs were set into place.

When the delivery men finished, Leah left Bobby with Reece to go collect the new bedding from the dryer. Bobby was crawling under the big bed when she came back. To her surprise, Reece helped her fit the bed ruffle and mattress pad, then helped her put the sheets on the bed. He even tucked in the bottom of the top sheet at the foot of the bed on his side, doing an impressive imitation of her crisp folds as he did.

The bed pillows got new cases, then the bedspread went on. Bobby chortled from beneath the bed and stuck his head out from under the dust ruffle to get Leah's attention. She bent down to respond and he giggled through a lighthearted game of peekaboo.

The warm sense of family and shared tasks might have been overlooked by most other people, but for Leah those simple moments were precious. Something inside her began to relax and feel warm and satisfied. A faint sense of permanence slipped through her but then was gone before she had little more than a scant second to recognize it.

Leah straightened and glanced over automatically at Reece, who stood on the other side of the big bed. His dark eyes were somber, and his rugged face gave nothing more away. She realized he'd been staring at her for a time, including those moments she'd crouched down to play peekaboo.

What had she done to make him stare? Had what they'd done that day just dawned on him and now seemed extreme? Was he having second thoughts?

Leah knew she could torture herself indefinitely with those questions. Overall, the day had been a pleasant one that made her feel a little more optimistic about the future. She hadn't expected that, but even if she was making too much of the day, she didn't want to lose the feeling yet.

''You look...thoughtful,'' she said, then made herself give him a small smile. ''Did you just realize how big a dent we made in the Waverly net worth?''

Something shot through his dark gaze and he tipped his head back the smallest fraction as if to study her from a slightly different perspective.

''I was thinking that you're beautiful. I was wondering why I never saw it so clearly until now.''

He paused, and it was just as well he did because what he'd said was such a shock that Leah needed to remember how to breathe.

''Like last night with your hair,'' he said almost absently. ''I've been looking at you for months. Years maybe. I don't know who I thought I was looking at, but it wasn't you.''

Leah couldn't maintain eye contact with Reece. She didn't know what to think of the stunning things he'd just said, much less think of a way to answer them or to even acknowledge them. The excruciating shame of a lifetime crept up.

Beautiful was the last thing she was, and she couldn't imagine why Reece would say that. She knew he wasn't a cruel man, so she knew he'd not said it because he'd meant it as some kind of sarcasm.

Was he trying to convince himself that she had the look of a woman he should have married? Rachel had been an uncommon beauty, and it was a fact that Leah was not.

''I think maybe the lighting in here needs to be turned up,'' she said, trying to make a joke of it before she rushed on. ''I need to cut the drawer liners so we can get your clothes switched. I can move my things in after supper.''

She hesitated a moment, still unnerved by what he'd said and even more jangled by his silence now. ''If you're still certain you want me to. Last chance to change your mind.''

Bobby chose that moment to crawl from under the bed on his daddy's side.

''Daddeee, gimme up.''

Reece ignored the baby. He was still staring over at her and she went breathless again waiting for him to say something about her offer.

''Daddeee, gimme up. Please!''

The high little voice seemed to break Reece's concentration, so he picked Bobby up.

''Gimme up, huh?'' he growled, and the sparkle of humor and love in his eyes as he gave the boy a tickle was as gently affectionate as Leah had ever seen. "I'll 'gimme up.'"

With that, he pretended to toss the boy through the air to the center of the big mattress, managing to catch Bobby to slow his descent and have him land with a soft bounce.

Reece pressed his big fists on the mattress to bounce the boy several times, and Bobby giggled with delight. Leah couldn't help but smile, though she was aware that Reece still hadn't commented on what she'd said. And the longer he took to do it, the more she began to believe that what he had to say wasn't good.

Reece stopped bouncing the child, who was still giggling, then picked him up and swung him to the floor.

Bobby protested that immediately. "Daddeee, gimme up!"

"It's your mama's turn to 'gimme up,' son." The little boy grinned over expectantly at her.

Reece put one knee on the mattress and stretched out his hand to her.

''Come on, Mama, let's see if this bed was worth the price.'' The sparkle of humor and affection that lingered in his gaze now had a glint of challenge mixed in.

Leah put out her hand, then thought better of it and started to pull back. Reece caught it anyway and in seconds he had them both on the bed, with Leah lying in his arms while he leaned over her. His voice was a warm growl.

''The last thing I'm gonna do is change my mind, Leah.''

And then his head descended and his lips settled forcefully on hers. Almost immediately, he deepened the kiss. The shock of the small invasion made her gasp.

Though she was too vastly inexperienced to be sure, Reece made this kiss feel as if he was staking claim to her, and she was helpless to keep from putting her arms around him. The carnal mating his mouth gave hers was beyond anything she'd expected, but then he mellowed the kiss and somehow drew her into matching his aggression.

His big hand began a sensual exploration of its own that made her shiver with new surprise before she melted every place he touched. She suddenly couldn't get enough of the wild tumble of sensation though she was nearly drowning in it.

Somewhere in the distance, she heard Bobby's voice, but it wasn't until Reece reluctantly lifted his mouth from hers and his hand moved away that she began to realize Bobby had managed to pull himself onto the bed and was climbing on Reece's back.

It was remarkably painful to have the kiss stop so suddenly, and she lay there in the aftermath trembling as she slowly became aware that Reece's big body was also trembling. She saw the harshness of frustration on his rugged face though his dark eyes sparkled with amusement at the boy's antics.

He was gentle with Bobby and shifted himself away slightly as he reached back to pull the boy around and tuck him between them. Bobby was delighted.

"Daddeee, gimme up."

Reece chuckled, though it sounded a little strained. "You mean bounce. But we might be done bouncin' baby boys for one day."

"Bouws, Daddee, bouws!"

Leah smiled a little, still dazed as she waited for the world to stop spinning. Bobby grabbed a handful of Reece's shirt to pull himself into a sitting position between them.

"I think you started something," she told Reece.

"Are you talkin' about the boy or you?"

Leah looked over into the smoldering lights in Reece's dark eyes. "I'd meant Bobby, but yes. I didn't expect that."

"Neither did I, but it was a fine taste."

Bobby reclaimed Reece's attention, and Leah took the opportunity to roll away and slide to the edge of the bed. She sat there a moment, waiting to feel a little less weak before she stood up. Reece had rolled to his back to lift Bobby into the air. It was a game they called "airplane" and it was clear that Bobby was wound up.

"If you wouldn't mind keeping him occupied, I'll get the drawers lined," she said.

"Go on ahead," he said as he took Bobby and rolled off the bed. "I'll see what I can do to get this one calmed down."

Leah was on her way out of the bedroom to find a pair of scissors, when the distant chime of the doorbell sounded.

"I'll get it," Reece said, then carried the squealing baby under his arm like a football and followed Leah out into the hall. Leah opened the linen closet after Reece and Bobby passed her, then found the scissors and returned to the bedroom.

She'd just started unrolling the drawer liner when she heard Reece call out for her. Leah checked her hair in the dresser mirror, surprised that she hadn't thought of that right away.

And she should have, because her barrette was askew and her hair was about to tumble free. She ended up rushing through Bobby's room to hers, then took a hasty few moments to brush out the length and rapidly put it back up.

In the stronger light of her bathroom, she could see that her face was flushed and her lips were puffy. She looked as if she'd just been given the kiss of her life. Although she had been and she'd loved every moment of it, Leah was more than a little appalled that she'd now have to face company.

She turned off the bright light, then hurried through her bedroom to the hall.

CHAPTER SIX

LEAH heard Margo Addison's voice just as she neared the end of the hall nearest the living room. Margo was Rachel's mother, but other than coloring, mother and daughter had had precious little in common.

"The boy always does that, Reece. It's not good that he's picked up her shyness."

Leah stopped, fully aware of who *her* was. Though Rachel and Leah had been best friends since their sophomore year of high school, Margo had objected relentlessly. The glamorous snob had been appalled that her beautiful, popular daughter had made a friend of a homely nobody who'd had the added notoriety of being a foster child from a white trash background.

Rachel, of course, had defied her mother and continued their friendship anyway, inviting Leah to parties or picking Leah up in her own car so she could either participate in school-related extracurricular activities or do things with other friends. They'd even studied together, because Leah got better grades. Leah had been happy to tutor her friend, who wasn't particularly attentive in class, because it was a way she could repay Rachel's friendship.

Though Leah had often suspected that Rachel had initially chosen to befriend her because she knew her snobbish mother would have a fit, Rachel soon proved herself to be a loyal and genuine friend.

Reece's low voice made Leah refocus on the conversation. "Leah does a fine job with the boy, Margo. He's just not used to you." Margo's Southern belle tone was saccharine.

"Why, of course she's doing a wonderful job with the boy."

Leah grimaced because she'd had years to know Margo would make a token agreement but then make her point anyway.

"It's just that children pick up the oddest things. Have you reconsidered hiring a nanny? The exposure would be so beneficial to the boy. And I've managed to hear of two very fine candidates. Both have such well-rounded, educated upbringings, so either of them could make certain Robbie's exposed to a variety of educational and cultural experiences that he might not otherwise have."

Reece's voice went lower. "My son is exposed to everything his parents mean for him to be exposed to." Leah picked up the faint warning in that and felt herself relax a little.

She'd weathered Margo's often hateful private comments to her from the beginning of this marriage, but she'd never before overheard anything Margo might have said to Reece when she was out of the room. She'd assumed it was going on, because Margo regarded Leah as a stain on her otherwise pristine life.

It touched her to have this proof that Reece defended her, whether she was present to know about it or not. She'd rarely worried that he'd be influenced against her by the things Margo might say to him in private, because she already knew what he thought of his former in-laws. He'd felt so strongly about them in fact, that he'd been willing to do anything to prevent his son from ever being raised by Margo, and to ensure that the boy's ranching inheritance was secure. It was the main reason he'd married Leah.

"Why, of course, dear," Margo went on, "I thought I'd mention it in case you—*and* Leah—change your minds. I'll continue to keep an eye out as Robbie gets older."

Robbie. Margo's persistent use of that name always set Leah's teeth on edge. Margo had made clear to her daughter before the boy was born that she not only disapproved of the name Robert but also disliked the nickname Bobby because it was so common. Referring to Bobby as Robbie better satisfied her sensibilities.

Leah felt guilty for hovering out of sight in the hall and silently moved back a few steps before she started forward, knowing her footsteps would now be heard. She steeled herself as she stepped out of the hall and walked into the big living room. As if Bobby hadn't seen her all day, he scrambled off his father's lap and toddled over to her.

Leah automatically bent down to pick him up, then carried him over to hand him back to Reece.

''Hello,'' she said, making herself smile pleasantly at Margo and her equally elitist husband Neville. Neville usually let Margo do most of the talking, but only because she spoke for both of them. "Can I get the two of you something cool to drink? We have iced tea and soft drinks."

Margo's green eyes sliced over her critically. Leah knew her cotton shirt and jeans were another indication to Margo of her low class background. Margo wore her perfectly tinted red hair styled to within an inch of its life and her white designer dress was the very height of summer fashion.

"I think I'd prefer something stronger...dear." The fractional hesitation was deliberate.

Leah glanced at Reece. "Would you mind?" She didn't serve liquor to anyone. Her family and her childhood had been destroyed by alcohol, and her personal bias was so strong that she'd have nothing to do with it.

Yes she knew Reece kept liquor in the house and that he sometimes had a drink, but she merely dusted the cabinet and the bottles and kept the glassware clean. The fact that Margo knew all about Leah's bias and the reason for it accounted for her request. And she made that particular one every time she and Neville stopped by. Because Leah had never discussed it with Reece, she had no idea whether he realized what was really going on or not.

Until she saw the perceptive glimmer in his dark gaze before he looked over at Margo.

''What would you like, Margo? Neville?'' Reece got to his feet and automatically passed Bobby back to Leah.

''A vodka for me. What would you like, Neville?'' she said to her husband. Before Neville could answer, she looked back at Reece. ''Make that two.''

Reece started for the den, and Leah went to one of the armchairs and sat down with Bobby. Instead of keeping the boy on her lap, she set him on the floor.

''Why don't you find your blocks? Maybe your grandmother and grandfather would like to see you build something.''

Bobby stuck a finger in his mouth and thought about that. Leah pointed to the lamp table nearby that had a basket beneath that was half full of alphabet blocks. Bobby looked toward them, then cast a shy gaze at Margo and Neville.

Leah's soft, ''Go on,'' prompted him walk partway there before he turned around and trotted back to climb into her lap.

''The boy's what? Fifteen months?''

Because Reece was no longer present to hear it, Margo's voice had lost its too sweet tone. Leah knew something was on its way.

She glanced over at Margo and smiled though it felt as fake as it probably looked. "Yes. Last week in fact."

"Have you taken him for his regular checkup?"

"He has an appointment next week," Leah answered, prepared for yet another small grilling session. Margo so bitterly resented that Leah had adopted her grandson that she never missed an opportunity to question Leah's competence.

The silence stretched and Leah let her gaze stray from the now silent, disapproving pair who sat on the sofa opposite her chair. She couldn't account for Margo's sudden silence, except she was probably saving up for Reece's return.

Nevertheless, it was a relief to hear Reece walk back down the hall and step into the living room with the drinks.

Margo took hers and thanked him profusely. Reece had just handed Neville his drink when Margo went on.

"It should be time for his measles-mumps-rubella. I hope someone's educated you about those."

Leah kept her smile firmly in place as Reece sat down. "I've read—"

"Have you quizzed the doctor about the wisdom of having each of those shots given separately? My physician tells me there's some concern about the usual practice of administering all three at once."

"As I said, I've read about them," Leah repeated calmly. "I also discussed the alternative with our doctor."

Margo's brow went up. "When was this?"

"At Bobby's last checkup."

"Well, I wouldn't mind going along to this next appointment," Margo said briskly. "I'd like to see for myself that this new young doctor is the person I want taking care of my grandson's medical needs."

Leah somehow maintained her polite expression. Margo's motive for doing that would be more to somehow harass or embarrass her than it would be for the good of the child, though neither of them would ever acknowledge that in front of Reece.

Reece spoke up. "Leah and I are satisfied with both the doctor's expertise and Bobby's care, Margo. There's no reason to concern yourself."

Reece's words had a finality that warned Margo that she was trespassing. He changed the subject.

"We're leaving in a few minutes to go to town for an early supper," he said. "Nothing fancy, just hamburgers and malts at the Lasso, but you're welcome to come along."

Though this was the first she'd heard of it, Leah was both relieved and amused by Reece's announcement. Margo and Neville had, in the past, dropped by just as Leah was about to put supper on the table. And since it wouldn't be polite not to invite them for the meal, she'd had to scramble to come up with impromptu vegetarian dishes.

Then, of course, she'd had to sit by and conceal her irritation when neither Margo nor Neville did more than push the food around on their plates.

Those times were always uncomfortable and aggravating for Leah, mainly because Margo was so adept at subtle digs and minor disagreements. Whatever the subject, she made a point of pressing Leah for her opinion, then immediately took the opposite view. She fussed over Bobby, but only to usurp Leah's care or to give condescending advice.

Leah had long since tired of such juvenile tactics, but she weathered them to keep the peace. She was aware of the fact that losing Rachel had devastated both

Margo and Neville, but because they were such remarkably cold people, it was easier for them to channel their grief into added resentment of her.

A small part of her had hoped that some of Margo's subtle digs might eventually penetrate Reece's distraction and provoke him as much as Leah was provoked. Apparently that time had come.

The Lasso was a small family-owned restaurant that neither Margo nor Neville would be caught dead in, so it was certain they'd decline the invitation. The fact that Reece had never taken Leah out to eat anywhere before yesterday made the sudden suggestion another nice surprise.

Margo recovered quickly from her shock and rallied. ''Ah, so our Leah is taking cook's night off. Good for you, dear. Preparing the same meals day in and day out would be wearing, I imagine. I've never understood why Reece didn't hire a new cook and housekeeper after the last one retired, but I imagine you enjoy keeping up your best skills.''

Margo barely took a breath before she glanced over at Bobby and coaxed brightly, ''Come here, Robbie. Give Grandmum a kiss before she goes home.'' She held out her manicured hands to the boy, then gave a little pout when Bobby turned his face shyly into Leah's shirtfront.

''It might help, Margo,'' Leah dared softly, ''if you called him Bobby.'' She saw the flash of surprise in Margo's eyes. One red-penciled brow arched high.

''Well, dear, that almost sounds like a...a criticism.''

Leah's calm, ''It's a suggestion,'' was the prelude to a brief silence. And then Neville stood up. That was apparently a signal to Margo who also stood.

''Well, we'll be going.'' Now she gave Bobby a wide smile and wiggled her fingers playfully. "Bye-bye, shy boy. Maybe next time you'll give your Grandmummy a nice welcome," she said before she added a singsong, "She'll bring you a present."

Thank heavens it was all over quickly then as Reece escorted them to the foyer then walked with them out to their car. Bobby immediately scrambled off Leah's lap and trotted over to the basket of blocks to drag it out from under the table.

When he had, he dug one out and held it up to declare, "Block!"

Leah leaned her head on the chair back and smiled. The child was himself again. "That's right. Would you like to bring them into the bedroom while Mommy finishes the drawers?"

She got up and helped Bobby carry the basket of blocks through the house to the master bedroom. He decided to line the blocks up along the edge of the new bed, so she got busy with the drawer liners and quickly finished. She'd gotten a laundry basket out of the linen closet to begin the transfer of clothing from Reece's old drawers into the new ones when Reece found her in the hall.

Leah was wary of his harsh expression, but she knew right away she wasn't the cause of whatever he was irritated about. No doubt Margo had made a parting shot.

"You aren't doing laundry now are you?" he asked gruffly.

"No. I was going to start moving your clothes."

"Put the basket away. I'll bring the drawers in. No sense handling everything twice."

In short order, Reece had carried in the drawers and Bobby toddled over to inspect the neatly stacked folded clothing. She and Reece worked together in silence to quickly make the transfers before Reece carried the drawers back to the guest rooms.

Leah took a few moments to change Bobby's diaper, then led him back to the bedroom and encouraged him to put his blocks back in the basket.

"How about we get to town? We'll move your things later."

Leah smiled. "Good idea. I was waiting for you-know-who to begin asking for you-know-what. By the time we get there and order, he'll be more than ready to...you know."

Reece's stony expression cracked. "You-know-who and you-know-what. Wonder how long those'll last?"

"Not too long," she said her dark brows going up. "In case you missed it, he perked up the moment I said 'you-know-who,' so I think he's figured out more than we realize. We'll soon have to brush up on our spelling skills, no doubt."

Reece was smiling over at Bobby as the little boy dropped another block into the basket. His love and pride was evident and the harshness had completely smoothed from his face. He looked relaxed and he looked ruggedly handsome. Leah couldn't help that her heart gave a little leap of attraction.

They gathered up the baby then drove into town for supper. After the busy day, it was a treat to not have to cook and clean up. Bobby enjoyed the outing, and it was another minor event that gave Leah a pleasant feeling of family.

Few people had ever seen the three of them together in public, and it was clear when other restaurant patrons either waved or stopped by their table for a quick hello that Reece seemed slightly uncomfortable with the sudden attention, though he didn't remark on it.

Later, they drove home and Reece helped her move her things into the master bedroom. He participated when she gave Bobby his bath and helped dress the boy for bed and tuck him in. Afterward Leah collected her toiletries from her bathroom and found places for them in Reece's.

When she was finished, she unpinned her hair then unclipped her barrette. The activity that day had mostly distracted her from tonight, but her tension had been rising steadily for the past two hours. Though they'd spent the entire day preparing to share the same bed, it still seemed too soon.

It didn't help a lot to remind herself that they should have passed this point months ago. The fact that they were doing this now—and only because Reece had insisted—still seemed as radical and ill-advised as marrying him in the first place.

And then she remembered that kiss last night and the one this afternoon and felt herself tremble with a potent mix of fear and feminine excitement. Would he go slowly and wait for feelings to develop between them or would that matter to him? The moment she'd brought up the subject of divorce, he'd gone out of his way to oppose the notion.

Would he rush things in the bedroom in order to consummate the marriage? He could probably guess that taking that step might make it even more difficult for Leah to leave him.

And a man didn't necessarily have to be in love with a woman to have sex. Though Leah couldn't imagine it with a man she didn't love, she was inexperienced enough, and yes, she loved Reece enough, that she didn't know if she could resist if he decided to seduce her.

How could she raise the subject of delaying intimacy without sounding like a nervous virgin? How could you tell your husband that a few kisses were fine, but no more? Or that you were wearing a long nightgown to bed so you hoped he owned pajamas?

Would he really understand that her inexperience and natural shyness was particularly inhibiting when she thought of actual lovemaking?

Leah put the barrette and hairpins out of the way on the counter.

Be careful what you wish for...

The old saying made another taunting pass through her mind. She suddenly couldn't bear to completely move into Reece's space. Because she had a deep need to maintain whatever sense of privacy and autonomy she could, she picked up her soap and her shampoo then got her blow-dryer and one of her brushes out of the drawer to carry them back to her old room. She'd shower in there, at least tonight. After taking a moment to collect her long nightgown and robe from the new dresser drawer, she made a quick dash through Bobby's room.

The boy was fast asleep, and she knew Reece must be busy finishing up some of the paperwork he hadn't gotten to that day. If she hurried, he'd never know the difference.

It felt good to go through her nightly routine in the place that was so familiar. She'd loved the beautiful room she'd lived in all these months. The master bedroom was larger than this one and the new furniture was gorgeous, but Leah had already felt like a princess in the room she'd had.

She'd never lived in such luxury, not when she was growing up and not as an independent adult with a tiny apartment down on the town square, so it was hard not to feel nostalgic about this, however silly that was.

Leah finished with her shower, dried her hair, then put on her nightgown and robe. The soft yellow cotton gown with narrow straps was completely opaque and covered her down to her ankles, as did the light-weight matching robe that went over it. She belted the robe loosely at her waist, then collected her towels and put them in the hamper.

As she slipped back through Bobby's room to go to the master bedroom, the last thing she expected was to find Reece already there waiting for her.

She faltered to an uncertain halt when she saw him sitting in an armchair he must have carried in from one of the guest rooms. He'd slouched down in the big chair, his head leaned back against it, his long length supremely at ease. His dark gaze sparkled with male interest as it made a leisurely sweep down the front of her belted robe to linger on her bare feet.

Her own wide gaze made a tour of its own. He'd obviously just showered, probably while she'd been using the hair dryer. His dark hair was still a bit damp and he was wearing jeans that were zipped but not buttoned, and because he wore no shirt, she could see the superb muscle definition of his chest and that it was lightly dusted with dark hair. The sheer masculinity of him in the dimly lit, quiet room reached out and wrapped around her.

"Is using the shower in here a problem for you?"

Leah cringed inwardly at the question. "I'm...a little nervous. Kind of a...last time thing. Maybe. I don't think so."

The babbling answer made her face go hot, and she felt ridiculously adolescent. She couldn't take her eyes off Reece, and they felt as big as dinner plates.

She couldn't seem to recover from the sight of him sitting there slouched down, his muscled arms resting on the chair arms, his long, denim-clad legs bent at the knees. His feet were bare, too. The unbuttoned jeans gave her the sudden idea that he'd only put them on because he didn't own a pair of pajamas.

So then, of course, he wouldn't be wearing them to bed—either the jeans or pajamas. The fact that there was no telltale peep of underwear behind the open button made her heart race.

CHAPTER SEVEN

IT WAS stunning to remember that little more than forty-eight hours ago they'd been so estranged from each other that she'd felt compelled to approach Reece with an offer to divorce.

Since then, they'd gone through a series of small changes that felt like little earthquakes compared to the deadness of the nonrelationship they'd had before. All day today those small changes had been evolving into ever larger ones, but this last one—sharing a bed with him—now seemed far too dangerous and potentially disastrous to allow.

It was too soon, far too soon. Leah felt completely unable to cope with this, though she'd dreamed of Reece for years.

Romantic fantasies and nebulous desires bore no resemblance to the blatant sexual reality of a half-dressed Reece Waverly. And when you added the unbuttoned jeans and the strong sense of sensual peril, she felt every bit the untouched virgin she was.

Leah put her hands together in front of her waist, lacing her fingers together tightly to still their tremors as the silence between them began to feel heavy. She felt so self-conscious and awkward. At least she could still think of something to say.

"I hope my alarm clock won't disturb you. I often wake up before it goes off, so you might not hear it at all."

Leah pressed her lips closed on the nervous babble she'd been on the verge of and prayed for Reece to end the suspense.

"You're nervous," he remarked calmly.

"And you're not," she said back. "I'm sorry. This isn't such a big adjustment for you since you were...married before."

The small smile she forced had a sickly curve that she wasn't aware of. ''I'll try to be more adult about it.''

With that, she turned toward to the bed then hesitated. ''Which side do you prefer?''

''Either's fine. Take your pick.''

Leah walked to the side nearest the bathroom, since she'd put her alarm clock on that bedside table. She pulled down the bedspread and top sheet then untied the belt of her robe with fingers that felt hopelessly uncoordinated.

Taking off the robe to drape it across the foot of the bed felt even more awkward, and instead of laying it neatly as she'd meant, it landed in a twisted heap. She snatched it up and had another try with roughly the same result. A quick glance toward Reece told her he'd watched her every move with interest.

An edgy feeling of embarrassment and frustration made her suddenly irritable.

"For my next trick, I'll get into bed, then roll over and fall out onto the floor."

This time, she managed to lay the robe tidily across the foot of the bedspread. Reece chuckled, and she heard him get up.

"Are you always so obsessively neat?"

Leah glanced warily in his direction as he walked to his side of the bed. She was aware that there were no pajamas in sight and that he might be about to shuck his jeans. It was difficult to keep his question in mind.

"I appreciate order. It doesn't always take so much time to be neat," she said, referring to the robe. "Keeping order allows you to be lazy, actually. Small messes take small moments of time and effort to straighten, as opposed to big messes that can take hours. Not to mention the ambi-

tion it takes to face them. A little prepa-
ration makes up for itself in time saved.''

Oh Lord! The nervous little lecture
made her sound like a persnickety spinster
who starched her underwear and gave her
furniture the white glove treatment.

Now Reece grinned over at her flushed
face. ''Will you fold me away in a drawer
somewhere if I get too messy?''

Her flushed face grew painfully hot.
''I'm sorry. I sound obnoxious, don't I?''

''You sound scared to death.''

Her swift, ''I am,'' came out involun-
tarily and her pride took another solid hit.
''Why did we do this, Reece? And the expense today...'' She turned away and sat
down on the edge of the mattress, feeling
guilty and bitterly disappointed in everything, particularly in herself.

She felt the bed move slightly and went
so tense that her body ached with it.
Reece's big hand closed warmly on her

shoulder as she felt him settle on his side behind her.

"You're wound up tight, darlin'. Lay down here and I'll work out the knots."

Leah reflexively started to rise, but his strong hand kept her where she was.

"No better way for you to relax than to let me prove I can be trusted."

"You don't need to prove anything to me," she said, glancing back over her shoulder to see his skeptical look. "I can relax on my own. I'll be fine."

"Not tonight," he said grimly. "I'm not gonna lay down next to a coiled spring and wonder when it's gonna snap."

The no-nonsense look on his face shamed her. She felt like a complete ninny, and she knew Reece didn't suffer fools gladly.

Only because she was certain her nervousness had offended and aggravated him did she submit, and she reluctantly lay down on her stomach. She'd been careful to make certain the nightgown still covered her all the way to her ankles, so she turned her face away from Reece and squeezed her eyes closed.

Reece rose and set his knees on either side of her thighs before he gently drew the pillow from beneath her head. Leah couldn't suppress the delicate shiver when he gathered her long hair.

"Your hair is like silk," he said gruffly, and she somehow endured the sweet sensation of feeling him handle it. "You ought to wear it down more."

When he laid it aside and his hands finally settled warmly on her upper back, they felt big enough to span the width of her shoulders.

"Ever had someone work out the kinks before?" he asked as his fingers began to gently search out and probe the small areas of tension.

Her soft, "No," didn't sound at all definitive, though it was.

Leah couldn't remember not craving to be touched. Because the craving was so strong and because she knew she was particularly vulnerable to it, she'd kept herself so rigidly aloof from the mere opportunity that Bobby was almost the only person who'd ever been allowed to cross that line. Dancing with Hoyt Donovan had been a huge, huge thing for her, and now that seemed like nothing compared to this.

With Reece there was an entirely new and deeper dimension of touch, not only because of the sexual element but because she loved him so very much.

As his hands began their careful labors, Leah felt the full horror of that discovery. She'd loved him for years, yes, but she'd tried very hard these past weeks to numb herself to her feelings until loving him was an idea that she'd become slightly detached from.

Yet the intensity of it must have been creeping back over her the past two days, particularly with that kiss last night. The horror she felt suddenly was because it had just dawned on her that she'd never loved Reece as much as she did now.

"You're fightin' me, darlin'," he murmured, and she felt the dampness beneath her closed eyelids. The person she was really fighting was herself, though he'd never guess that.

She'd never considered herself self-destructive, but she wondered about it tonight. If she'd still possessed the strong will to survive that had taken her this far, she would have found the strength to throw Reece's hands off and fled to barricade herself behind a locked door. Or to have at least refused him and made it stick.

But the hard-palmed, callused hands and fingers that moved with such devastating authority on her body slowly spread an intoxicating magic that radiated everywhere. And then the diabolical gathering of heat in her most feminine places began and Leah knew this was the beginning of the end for her.

What Reece was doing would ensure that he could have whatever level of physical intimacy he wanted, whenever he chose for it to start, for however often and long he wanted it to go on. What amazed her now was how many years she'd managed to live without having the simple basic human need to be touched satisfied. Surviving so long without it was surely her own personal eighth wonder of the world. What Reece was doing to her now easily comprised the first seven.

As she entered that sensual twilight that wasn't quite sleep, Leah wondered dimly if Reece's heart was at least minimally involved in this. Or had everything these past forty-eight hours, particularly what he was doing now, simply been the practical action of a savvy, experienced man who wanted to keep his marriage intact?

Then again, maybe it wasn't so hard to decide what he was thinking about this or what he might really feel about doing it. Perhaps he'd given his answer long before she'd thought of the question.

I'm not gonna lay down next to a coiled spring and wonder when it's gonna snap.

Spoken, no doubt, by a tired man who'd much rather take a few moments to ensure a good night's sleep than a caring husband whose only motive was to give comfort to his wife.

And yet his unrushed hands conveyed anything but a lack of care. Leah was literally lulled to sleep by the sweet pleasure of his touch.

*   *   *

She awakened that next morning a dozen minutes before her alarm clock went off. The male warmth that pressed against her back from her head to her heels and the arm that rested heavily around her waist, created a sense of security and belonging that she'd rarely felt.

Loathe to move away, she lay quietly to savor it. Leah shifted her arm and cautiously laid it on top of Reece's. Though his arm was much longer than hers, she fitted her small hand over the hair-roughened back of his for a few moments. The hunger to explore while he wasn't awake to know it, made her lightly trace the veins and scars on the back of his hand.

Did she dare lace her fingers with his? Reece's slow, steady breath assured her he was still sleeping, so she gently slid her fingers between his and curled her fingertips into his hard palm.

Doing such silly, trivial things suddenly seemed tantamount to a mouse braiding the ruff of a sleeping lion. Lions didn't appreciate braids, particularly when they woke up to find prey within reach. Playing finger-patty with a virile man who'd been celibate for nearly year and a half might be appreciated in a way she wasn't ready for if her exploration woke him up and he realized the opportunity to end his celibacy lay trapped beneath the weight of his arm.

Better to stop the foolishness and slip out of harm's way. An experimental move made her aware that her nightgown had crept up in the night. The simultaneous realization—that Reece had worn neither jeans nor pajamas to bed—made it even more prudent to slip away.

Leah might have made it if Reece's arm hadn't flexed to drag her back solidly against him.

His voice was rusty from sleep. "You've still got four minutes."

Her soft, "But I'm awake now," made him chuckle.

"So am I."

With that, he rolled her to her back, then rose up on an elbow to loom over her. His dark eyes studied her face and she went breathless as his head descended.

His lips pressed so gently against hers that she felt the warmth of them wash through her in a sensual wave. The scratchy burr of his beard stubble added a rough texture she hadn't felt before, but the kiss was over too soon for her to decide if she liked it or not.

He drew back to growl, "Good morning," and she got out a shy "Good morning" to him.

He reached over to slide the switch on her alarm, probably the moment before it was due to go off. "Now you can go," he said and Leah couldn't miss the sparkle of humor in his dark eyes.

She rolled away from him to the edge of the bed then walked to the dresser for a bra and jeans before she went to the closet to collect a shirt to carry with her into the bathroom. When she'd finished with everything and come out, Reece had dressed and was waiting his turn.

Bobby was still sleeping soundly, so she rushed quietly to the kitchen to start breakfast. The world seemed to have shifted. Now as she went about meal preparations, there was a level of satisfaction and permanence that hadn't existed before, perhaps because she felt a little more like a wife than a cook and housekeeper this morning.

What about Reece? Did he feel a little more like a husband? Or did he merely feel relief because last night had helped put the question of divorce a little farther out of the picture?

Determined to keep her hope to a sensible level, Leah went about making breakfast to distract herself.

Reece went back to working outside, and Leah followed her normal morning routine. He'd not only reminded her of the bedroom set he'd given permission to donate, but he'd asked her to try to make arrangements today so he could have some of the men move it out and get it delivered.

A call to the pastor set everything else in motion, and he agreed to receive the furniture at the church in order to facilitate the anonymous donation Leah considered proper. The set would be delivered later that afternoon to the family who'd recently lost their possessions in a house fire.

The men came to move out the furniture after midmorning, and Leah was grateful to get that taken care of. Once they were gone, she took Bobby and hurried into the empty bedroom to give it the same thorough vacuuming as she had Reece's room. Since the men would stop back when they returned from town, she wanted things ready for them to move Reece's old set in.

By the time everything was done and she served lunch, Bobby was cranky enough for a nap. Leah finally gave up trying to get him to eat the little sandwich she'd cut into fancy shapes and let him have the cookie she'd meant to save for his dessert.

Reece had been silent through most of the meal and Leah wondered at that. At least at breakfast they'd talked over the arrangements for the furniture. Just a bit ago, Reece had come in, washed up and taken a moment to kiss his son, but once he'd sat down for grace and started eating, he'd seemed preoccupied. Not even Bobby's fussiness had done more than draw his gaze briefly.

Leah couldn't help wondering if they were back to business as usual. He'd kissed her that morning before she'd gotten out of bed, but there'd been nothing after that. Yes, he'd made eye contact with her, but there'd been no glimmer of interest and not so much as a shared touch between them.

It was suddenly hard to reconcile Reece's cool distance now with the profoundly sexy male who'd sat in that armchair last night and let his warm gaze wander lazily over her.

The emotional abandonment of her childhood and a lifetime of insecurity made it impossible to ignore the significance of this.

Leah got Bobby to drink the last of his milk, then reached for the damp washcloth to gently wash the cookie crumbs from his face and hands. When she finished, she set the cloth on the chair tray, then stood to unlatch it and lift the boy out.

"Tell Daddy you'll see him later," she said softly and Bobbie's fussing turned to tears.

"No nap, Mama, no!"

"Oh yes, sweet boy," she said with a soft chuckle of sympathy as she cradled him tenderly.

Reece glanced at her but his dark gaze slid so quickly from her to the baby that she couldn't miss the small rebuff. He reached over to give Bobby a soft pat on the back.

"Go on with your mama, do what she says."

Leah moved away from the table and carried the boy through the house to his room. She heard the soft chime of the doorbell, but ignored it since Reece was in the house.

After removing Bobby's shoes and changing his diaper, she put up the side of the bed. She lingered only long enough for Bobby to rub his eyes and turn onto his side. He was good about going right to sleep, so she moved out of the room.

Since she hadn't heard the doorbell a second time and Reece hadn't called her, she assumed whoever it was had either come to see Reece or was already gone.

Though she wasn't up to facing Reece's remoteness again, she needed to get things done in the kitchen. If they had a guest, it wouldn't be proper not to offer something to drink on a hot day. A quick pass by the kitchen and the living room showed her they were empty, so she went down the hall in the opposite wing of the house to the den to check there.

She heard Reece say something but didn't see Hoyt Donovan until she'd walked into the room.

"Well, amigo," Hoyt was saying, "now that we've got that outta the way, how'd you do with my advice about Leah the other night?"

The question impacted her like a slap and Leah came to a breathless halt. Hurt blossomed, followed quickly by a flash of anger so intense that she felt the heat of it scorch her face all the way to her hairline.

It was just after Hoyt had gone home that Reece had given her that soul-shattering, out-of-the-blue kiss in Bobby's room, followed by his insistence on sharing a bed. Too angry over the insight to be thinking straight, Leah spoke up.

"What advice was this, Mr. Donovan?" she asked, and had the satisfaction of seeing both men give guilty starts. "By the way, would you like something to drink? Iced tea?"

Hoyt seemed to fumble a bit, and that was unusual for a man who'd never been known to be a loss for words. He couldn't have confirmed her suspicion more emphatically had he made a full confession.

"Ah, well..."

Hoyt glanced toward Reece, then back to Leah. It was clear to her that Hoyt was trying to come up with a tactful way to word his answer that would be truthful and yet not completely accurate.

Leah made herself smile, though it probably looked as strained as it felt. "You don't have to answer that, Hoyt. I'm sure you meant well. Would you like the tea?"

"No. No thanks, Miz Leah. Don't wanna cause you the extra work."

"The tea is the least of the extra work I've done the past two days," she said, unable to keep her gaze from straying to Reece's stony expression. She was bursting with the need to say something to him, but the harsh reserve of lifetime was reasserting itself.

"If you change your mind about the tea, let me know."

With that, she turned away and walked from the room, her back rigid with angry pride. She stalked to the kitchen where she cleared away the lunch dishes with a ferocity that finished the task in record time.

In truth, she was more angry with herself than she was with Reece. He'd genuinely adored Rachel, and Leah couldn't fault him for not being able to find something in his heart for her, but it was excruciating to wonder how hard it had been for him to go through the motions.

Leah finished wiping the counter before she draped the dishcloth over the faucet and washed her hands. When she finished, the muddle she'd made of everything crowded in and she leaned dispiritedly against the counter.

Perhaps something had been accomplished after all. Perhaps now Reece understood in a way that he hadn't before that kissing a woman and sharing a bed with her, along with all the other inconsequential things they'd done the past two days, weren't things that he could continue putting himself through indefinitely.

After all, he'd lived the real thing. He, more than she, ought to be particularly repelled by the idea of forcing himself to go through the motions with her after the passionate romance he'd had with Rachel.

Because he'd been as remote from her today as before, he must have realized that already. Her heart seized the idea and she felt bitterly certain. And it hurt to know how quickly he'd come to that conclusion.

A prickling at the back of her neck got her attention and she lifted her head to glance over her shoulder.

The surprise of seeing Reece standing a few feet away with his feet braced apart and his arms crossed over his chest, startled her badly. She let go of the counter edge and turned jerkily to face him.

CHAPTER EIGHT

HOYT was nowhere in sight, so he must have hightailed it for home. Leah couldn't blame him. One look at the stormy expression on Reece's face and Leah suddenly wished she had someplace safe to escape to herself. No sense pulling any punches.

"This won't work, Reece. You know it already, don't you?" Her voice was remarkably steady considering her heart had jumped into her throat.

"The hell it won't," he groused.

Leah's gaze shied from his. "I'm clearly not the right woman for you. If I were, things between us the past two days would have happened naturally. You wouldn't have needed someone to list things for you to do, and you wouldn't have had to... force them.''

''You're wrong.''

His gruff words were a pronouncement that she was compelled to challenge.

''How am I wrong? Hoyt gave you advice, you decided to take it. We had a couple of kisses and we've slept in the same bed. I think you realize you can't go on like this.''

Reece's gaze wavered from hers momentarily and he let out a harsh sigh. When his gaze came back to hers it had softened. So had his voice.

''I know what you heard and it's plain your feelings were hurt. I admit Hoyt hands out plenty of advice to folks who don't ask for it, but if you think I had to force myself to do a damned thing I've done with you, then you're blind. As a bat.''

She shook her head, not believing him. ''Oh, Reece.'' She paused when she saw the flare of anger in his eyes. ''I'll stay with you as long as you want me here, but please don't force things because you think I'll leave if you don't.''

''You think I forced myself to kiss you?'' Reece unfolded his arms and looked faintly amused.

Leah studied him warily. ''I don't know, but I can't stand to think you might have. And you've been distant again today—and unhappy—like before. It's not that I expected grand romantic gestures, but I do know when you've put up no trespassing signs.''

Reece gave her a narrow look. ''You wanna know why I've been standoffish today, or would you rather keep jumping to conclusions?''

Leah couldn't maintain eye contact with the harsh probe of his gaze and looked away. She leaned back against the counter and crossed her arms, resigned. ''I suppose.''

Reece started her way and she looked up. He reached her just as she straightened from the counter. Just that fast, his hands spanned her waist. Before she realized what he was doing, he lifted her to the counter next to the sink. She'd grabbed his shoulders reflexively and now she kept her hands there. She felt a fierceness in him and her instinct was to keep him at a distance if need be.

His rugged face was stern and his gaze was turbulent. ''You sure you wanna hear this?''

Leah gave a hesitant nod.

''I want you to stay, and I'm getting what I want,'' he said, then added tersely, ''so far.''

He paused, his grip easing only a bit on her waist though he didn't release her.

"Because I'm getting that much, all I've been able to think about today is how long it's been since I've had sex."

Her gaze shied from his at the stark declaration, and she felt her face go hotter. Reece flexed his fingers on her waist to prompt her to look at him. When she did, she saw that his gaze was smoldering now. His low voice went gravelly.

"I don't trust myself not to take you to bed while the boy's taking his nap." The harshness on his face seemed to amplify his utter bluntness as he added, "You deserve more than to be rushed just because I'm burning up."

Leah was so shocked she couldn't move.

"That explain it for you?" His tone was just short of belligerent.

Her soft "yes" did little to temper the fiery lights in his dark eyes. She wanted to do more than just rest her hands on his wide shoulders, but Reece was so tense that the cotton-covered flesh beneath her palms felt like iron. His dark brows lowered in a surly frown.

"Now what's wrong?"

Leah couldn't help the nervous giggle that came gurgling up. "I'm afraid to move."

She felt some of Reece's tension ease away as he made a sound that was part growl and part chuckle. He leaned close, hovering a scant inch from her mouth before his lips seized hers and he pulled her to the edge of the counter.

When she felt him fit his hips snugly between her thighs, Leah's shock was quickly swept away beneath the aggressive possession of his mouth. She clutched at him, and the sharp desire she felt wrung a soft moan from her.

Just when she thought she might not survive the dizzying wonder of his mouth and now his hands, Reece began to temper the kiss. Far too soon, his mouth shifted off hers and his arms closed even more tightly around her.

He was trembling, and Leah felt a stir of feminine power. Reece's heart was beating even harder than hers, and it pounded them both. He pressed his lips fervently into her hair then nuzzled her neck for several breath-stealing moments more before he started to pull away.

"Ease up on me, lady," he said hoarsely. "At least while it's daylight."

He studied her flushed face then his gaze lifted to her hair before dropping back down to her kiss-swollen lips.

"Find something quiet to do. Let me go back to paperwork and forget you're in the house."

Leah stared, still a little dizzy. Reece had never looked harsher, he'd never looked more masculine and powerful. Everything feminine in her was completely overwhelmed and thoroughly attuned to him. There was nothing faked or insincere about any of this, and she doubted she'd ever think so again.

Reece lifted her down then pulled away to turn and stalk from the kitchen without a backward glance. Leah sagged against the counter because her legs barely held her up.

It was much later, probably late afternoon, before it dawned on Leah that there was a world of difference between the kind of love she so craved and what Reece had been talking about. It distressed her to realize that for all that time, the difference hadn't mattered to her at all.

And he hadn't mentioned waiting until he felt something for her, only that all he could think about was sex and that she didn't deserve to be rushed. Once again, the emotional consequences of what she'd gotten herself into seemed endless.

*　　*　　*

The moment Reece saw his wife at supper, he knew he'd confessed too much that afternoon. She was the standoffish one now. He sensed her unease and it made him feel like a sex-crazed animal.

Leah was more sensitive than Rachel and so much more fragile and vulnerable. He'd automatically compared Leah to Rachel out of habit, and in the past he'd done it in a way that made Leah seem second best, if that. But there was a depth to Leah that intrigued and drew him, an untouched naïveté and wary innocence that seemed both sweet and sad.

He felt almost as tender toward her now as he did toward Bobby, and that got his attention. Any notion of second best was gone and he wasn't sure when it had happened.

Like noticing how long her hair was the other night and how pretty her eyes were, and yesterday, how subtly beautiful she was. Subtly beautiful, because Leah's wasn't the kind of beauty that struck you at first sight as Rachel's had, but the kind of beauty that dawned more slowly then repeatedly drew and held the eye. The kind of beauty that went deeper and far outlasted the kind that spanned a handful of years then began to fade.

And this was the woman who'd taken such fine care of him and his son all these months. The goodness and generosity in the countless things she'd done had conferred a beauty all their own.

Leah deserved so much more than she'd gotten so far. As he cut himself another piece of steak, he decided to do something about the silence between them.

"What do you do when Bobby's with me in the evenings?"

Leah looked his way. "I read or watch a movie. Or there's some little chore to take care of. Sometimes I go for a walk."

"You can go anywhere on this ranch, you know," he said as he caught the piece of steak on his fork tine. "Take one of the pickups if you want. Just tell someone where you're going. Same thing if you want to go riding."

She looked down at her plate and pushed at a lima bean. "It's been a long time since I've gone riding. I'm probably not very good at it anymore."

"It'll come back to you fast enough. I'll take you with me some morning while it's cool."

Her quiet blue gaze came up to meet his and he could tell she liked that idea. "I'd have to find someone who'd take Bobby that early."

"Maggie'd be a good one for early mornings," he said, referring to his foreman's wife. "Why not call her after supper? We'll go the first morning she can do it."

Leah nodded, feeling a little more at ease. Bobby tried to shift his plate off his chair tray, but she calmly reached over to take it. Reece went on.

''I reckon we're overdue to find someone to help out around here anyway,'' he said. ''If you had more time to yourself, going out early with me wouldn't be complicated. We can hire whoever you like.''

Leah set Bobby's plate out of harm's way on the table but didn't comment. She'd loved having a home to take care of, and she'd taken enormous pride in that. She knew she wasn't very modern that way, but she'd never been very sophisticated or particularly obsessed with the notion of a career, particularly when having a home and a family was something she'd hungered for her whole life.

''I never meant for you to handle everything single-handedly after Ina retired,'' he went on. ''I think I brought that up a couple times over the months, but Bobby's getting older. And things are changing between us.''

Leah searched his face as he looked down and finally took the bite of steak he'd just cut. His was a common sense suggestion, but another adjustment. A big one, since one of the things that Leah had been grateful for the past eleven months was that everything between them had been completely private. Without a live-in housekeeper, there'd been no one around to witness the stark emotional and physical distance between them, much less discover they'd slept in separate beds all this time.

She wasn't certain yet how much things would actually change between them, so the last thing she wanted was to bring a stranger in. The potential for gossip was something she was leery of.

''I'll think about it,'' she said at last, passing Bobby his cup.

Reece frowned and finished with the bite of steak. She looked down at her plate but felt his scrutiny and knew he was impatient with her answer.

''I've got people who can handle things for me, Leah,'' he persisted. ''It's only fair for you to have people who can handle things for you. To free up your time.''

Leah looked over at him, compelled to point out the critical difference. ''But your people don't sleep under this roof, and they aren't in the house all day and night like a housekeeper would be.''

She was thinking of that afternoon when Reece had come to the kitchen. The idea that a housekeeper might have accidentally walked in on that made her queasy. After all, she'd walked into the den at an awkward moment herself when Hoyt had been here.

She saw a flicker of something in Reece's gaze that suggested he'd just thought of the same thing.

"So find someone to work part-time," he told her. "No law says we have to have a live-in like Ina. Truth to tell, now that I've done without live-in help all these months, I'm not sure I'm as fond of the idea anymore."

Leah relaxed a little at the compromise, pleased that Reece had proposed it. "I didn't grow up with housekeepers and cooks, so having them isn't important to me. But you're right about Bobby. He's becoming more and more active, so it might be nice to have someone come in for a day or two a week. I'll ask around and see who might be available."

"Good. Do the things you like and leave the rest to whoever you hire. Later on, if you decide you want more than a day or two of help, add more days. Add a whole week. Move them into the house. It's up to you, since this house is your territory."

It was a typically chauvinist remark and Leah suppressed a sudden smile, amused by it rather than insulted. And because she'd thoroughly enjoyed taking care of this house and was proud of how well she'd done with it, the remark was as much an acknowledgment of that as it was a declaration that she had a place of authority on Waverly Ranch, however modest others might consider that.

Even Rachel might have laughed at how unliberated that was, but Rachel had never known anything but privilege and security, and she'd managed to always get her way wherever she went. For someone who'd never really had a home of her own other than her small apartment, much less any sort of authority over it, being in charge of the Waverly ranch house was akin to ruling a small kingdom.

Reece finished with his steak and reached for his glass of iced tea. Leah noted that and set down her fork.

"I made dessert. Nothing fancy, just a no-icing corn cake sprinkled with powdered sugar. Unless you'd rather have it with coffee later."

"How much did you make?"

"Just a small pan."

Reece grinned over at her and she felt the warmth of it to her toes. "Enough for now and later on?"

Leah smiled, flattered. Now that Reece was paying attention, he wasn't shy about expressing his appreciation. "Both if you like."

"Both, then. I can get it. Where's it at?"

"In the top oven," she said, amazed at the sense of closeness his offer gave, though she knew it was silly to confer so much on such a small thing.

Reece got up and walked to the double ovens to get out the small cake plate and carry it to the table. He stopped by the counter where she'd set out the dessert plates and a serving spatula. By the time he sat down, Leah had refilled their tea glasses and added a small measure of milk to Bobby's cup.

Bobby had been fairly quiet at supper that night, but he lit up when he saw the cake. ''Kay, kay!''

Reece served them all, then had a taste of the modest dessert. After he had, he fixed her with a faintly cranky look.

''Is cooking and baking one of the things you'll be sharing with hired help?''

Leah had just taken a sip of her tea and now set the glass down. ''Probably not, but would you like me to?''

''Hell, no.''

Leah smiled, but then discretely pointed at Bobby who was putting a pinch of cake into his mouth. ''Oops, Daddy.''

Reece immediately assumed a penitent expression though his dark eyes were laughing. ''Thanks much, Mommy. I'll watch my language. Good cake.''

''I'm glad you like it,'' she said, then had a taste of her own.

Their table conversation hadn't been scintillating or witty or brilliant, but the deep down happiness it caused felt sweet. The two people she loved most in the world were with her. One she knew loved her completely because she was the woman he'd grow up thinking of as his mother. The other at least liked her as a friend again, and he'd made it clear he wanted her to remain in his life. And he desired her. There had to be at least some caring in those things, something that might grow into a bit more.

After dessert, Reece took care of washing Bobby's face and hands while Leah cleared the table and loaded the dishwasher. He whisked Bobby away for a fresh diaper, then brought him back just as she finished.

''How 'bout that walk?'' he asked, and Leah was again struck by the pleasure of having him ask.

They took a leisurely walk down to the stables in the warm evening. Bobby toddled along with them, and they paused whenever he stopped to look at something. Reece caught her hand and Leah felt the dizzying thrill of his warm grip.

They looked at some of the horses in the stable, and Reece led his sorrel gelding out of a stall. He put Bobby on the big horse's bare back, and then put a cautious hand on the boy's leg as he walked the horse down the stable aisle and back. Bobby clung to a hank of red mane and enjoyed every moment of the ride.

When it was over, Reece lifted him off and set him on the ground. Bobby immediately howled his protest.

"Gimme up, gimme up!" Huge tears shot down his pink cheeks and he stamped his little feet in a truly impressive temper tantrum.

Leah and Reece exchanged shocked looks, then tried not to laugh. Reece straightened to his full height and forced himself to glare down sternly at his small son.

"Bobby, that's enough."

The snap of authority in Reece's low voice got Bobby's attention, and Leah felt her heart squeeze at the sight as the tiny boy abruptly went silent and looked up, round-eyed, at his towering father.

"That's better. Come here." Reece reached out to guide the child closer to the horse. "Tell Boss goodnight."

Bobby lifted his little hand and waggled his small fingers. "Ni-night."

The massive horse stretched his nose toward the boy to blow his warm breath against him. Bobby giggled and reached eagerly for the horse's big head.

''Gimme up!''

Reece held him back and gave a low, ''Not now. Give him a pat and we'll let him go night-night.''

Leah couldn't help her grin at the sound of Reece's gruff voice as he repeated Bobby's babyish ''night-night.'' In the next moment the swift stab of love she felt made her eyes sting.

She looked on blurrily as Reece patiently guided the little boy's hand to the horse's nose for a few gentle strokes.

''Ni-night, hose,'' Bobby said solemnly, and Reece shot Leah a grin.

She wondered if the reason the little one was so somber with his goodnight might be because he was thinking about how near his own bedtime was. She looked on as Reece set the boy on the other side of the stable aisle.

"Stand right there," he said with gentle sternness before he turned back to the big horse and led him into the stall.

Leah watched to make certain Bobby stayed where he was until the horse was put away and Reece walked out to shut the stall gate. Bobby rushed over to him and Reece plucked him off the floor to lift him to his shoulders.

They walked together toward the ranch house, and Bobby chattered, still wound up over his ride. Reece set him on his feet when they got to the back patio. He and Leah sat together on the wide bench swing out back while Bobby played with his small collection of outdoor trucks.

Reece dropped his arm across her shoulders and pulled her tighter against his side. After a moment, he reached over and caught her left hand to gently examine her fingers.

"I didn't even get you a ring."

The remark was unexpected and Leah was instantly uncomfortable. She couldn't look at him.

"There were so many other things on your mind. On both our minds."

"Don't make excuses for me, Leah."

She lifted her free hand to put it over the back of his, unable to stop the gesture of fondness. She looked into his dark eyes.

"I'll do what I want," she dared softly. "And what would a ring have meant eleven months ago? It was difficult enough to cope with everything else."

His face went utterly grim and he looked down at their clasped hands. He gave hers a gentle squeeze, and his words came out in a low rumble.

"We're done skipping over things. We'll take care of the rings tomorrow."

She sensed his guilt and felt bad about it. "Please, Reece. We don't know—"

"*I* know, Leah," he said sternly, and looked at her. "This is for life. Unless you can tell me you don't feel anything for me and you doubt you ever will."

The sudden silence in the wake of his demand put her squarely on the spot and she mentally scrambled for words.

"I couldn't say either of those things," she said at last, unable to look away. She'd meant to be more evasive than that, but instead she'd revealed more than she'd meant to. She held her breath, hoping Reece hadn't realized that, but his steady scrutiny told her he had. Her gaze shied from his.

"Then we'll get those rings tomorrow." The subject was closed.

"It's time for Bobby's bath," she said as she pulled her hand from Reece's and quickly stood.

She felt him watch her every move as she helped Bobby stow his trucks under a patio bench. When Bobby trotted away from her toward the end of the patio opposite the house, Reece intercepted him. He tucked the wiggly little boy under his arm like a football and carried him into the house after Leah opened the door to the kitchen.

Though neither of them had mentioned the word ''bath'' or ''bedtime'' to the baby, by the time they walked into the hall to the bedrooms, Bobby started his usual protest.

''No baff, Mama. No ni-night.''

Reece chuckled. ''Can't put dirty boys to bed without a bath.''

''No ni-night!''

Reece swung the boy upright to carry him on his arm as they reached Bobby's room. Leah followed the pair as they crossed the carpet to the bathroom.

Once they'd got the baby's clothes and diaper off and Leah carried his little sneakers to empty them of the dirt he'd picked up on their walk, Reece took over Bobby's bath. She'd put the child's soiled clothes in the hamper and was standing by with a fluffy towel when Reece lifted him out of the tub onto the bath mat.

In no time at all, Bobby was dry and dressed for bed. Though he was now fighting sleepiness, he offered them both a round of kisses and sweet hugs before they put him to bed and retreated to the hall.

Reece's amused gaze met hers. "You'd best call Maggie before it gets late," he reminded her. "I've got a couple of things to finish up in the den, then I'll be ready to turn in."

There was another message beneath the words and Leah felt the sultry whisper of it. She thought immediately of what he'd said that afternoon about sex and burning up, and felt her cheeks heat.

Reece hadn't shown a single sign of the masculine fierceness he'd had in the kitchen that day, so her tension had ebbed completely away. Now it came rolling back and brought with it a feminine anticipation that was part dread and part excitement.

It was too soon for that level of intimacy and yet she felt the potent lure. For a woman who'd come to believe she'd never have even a few of the things they'd shared the past few days, she couldn't help craving more. Surely Reece couldn't be intimate with her and keep his heart completely remote?

"Something wrong?"

Leah automatically shook her head and forced herself to smile.

"Maybe just shy about calling Maggie," she said, relieved to think of something truthful. "I haven't talked to her for a few days, and I've never asked her to keep an eye on Bobby. I usually hire Marie, since she does day care in town.''

Though she could see the watchfulness in Reece's gaze, he seemed to accept her explanation.

''Might want to see if Maggie'd like to do it on a regular basis for pay here at the house.''

''That's a good idea.''

They went their separate ways after that, and Leah was grateful for the time alone. Maggie agreed to come to the house and watch Bobby any morning Leah liked, since she was always up as early as Leah was to cook her husband's breakfast. And she was very interested in watching Bobby on a regular basis for pay, though she'd wanted to think about it.

Maggie often hired on as an extra ranch hand at different times of the year, particularly foaling time. She was a quilter, and donated a lot of her time to local 4H

groups. She and Jim had two grown sons
who were living on their own, so she'd had
vast experience with little boys. It would
be a wonderful match.

Leah checked on Bobby to make certain
he'd gone to sleep, then crossed to the connecting door to step into the silent master
bedroom. She switched on a lamp, unable
to keep from glancing toward the huge bed
as her tension jerked up a few extra
notches.

CHAPTER NINE

LEAH brushed her teeth and took her first shower in the master bath before she dressed in her nightgown and dried her long hair. Though she'd made too much noise to hear whether Reece had come into the bedroom or not, she assumed he had. He'd showered before supper tonight as he most often did, and it was getting late. Since they got up just after four in the morning, a nine p.m. bedtime was the norm.

By the time she turned off the bathroom light and came out, Reece was sitting up in bed with a pillow wedged between his back and the headboard. He'd brought in a stock magazine and was thumbing through it, but his dark gaze shifted to her and went somber as it fixed on her face, then her hair before it made a lingering sweep of the rest of her.

"I should have come in when you did earlier. I haven't had the pleasure yet of takin' your hair down." He leaned his head back against the big headboard to give her a lazy look. "I reckon I will soon enough though."

Leah couldn't help that her face felt warm. It was hard to keep from staring at Reece's wide, masculine chest and lean middle. He set his magazine on the bedside table then reached over to flip down her side of the bedspread and top sheet in a wordless invitation. She fumbled with the belt of her robe then slipped it off to drape it over the foot of the bed.

The quiet room was heavy with a low-level charge of expectation. It went without saying that there'd be no sexless massage tonight, not when Reece's dark gaze was virtually eating her up. Last night, she'd fallen asleep so quickly that she hadn't truly faced lying awake next to him at a time with the most potential for love-making.

Tonight she'd be awake, and her insides were knotting tighter with every wary beat of her heart. She got into bed and pulled the covers up. Reece slid down and turned onto his side to prop his jaw on a fist and look down at her. His other hand curled around her waist and his voice lowered to a rasp.

"I can feel your heart going a million beats a minute, Leah."

Her gaze shied from the gentle probe of his. She felt stiff, and she kept her hands folded primly on her middle because as idiotic as it was, she didn't know whether she should touch him or not. "I don't mean to be so nervous." An awkward smile burst up from the self-consciousness she felt. "I'm not very good at knowing what to do."

"What do you want to do?"

The question somehow pierced deep, landing someplace so lonely and lost and afraid that the words were out of her mouth before her brain could catch them. "I'd like to feel free but be safe, not so tied up inside." Once that much had come out, she took a shaky breath and let herself say the rest. "I don't want to make the wrong choices, Reece. I'm...terrified this is all a big disaster in the making."

It probably qualified as one of the biggest confessions of her life, and she laid there a little in shock to realize how easily it had slipped out in the beginning, and yet how easy it had been to decide to include the rest of it. A huge wave of emotion surged up from the turmoil of nerves and longing she felt.

Reece lifted his hand from her waist and caressed her flushed cheek. The light touch sent a shower of tingles through her.

''We're done with disasters, you and I.'' The solemnity in his dark eyes was powerfully persuasive, and Leah couldn't seem to help falling prey to it. ''We've gone too long without being close. Time to change that.''

And then his dark head descended and his cool lips eased gently onto hers. He retreated a hairbreadth as if waiting for some signal from her. She lifted her hands to tentatively touch his bare chest with her palms and fingertips.

Leah felt the shudder that went through him before his lips seized hers and his arms slid around her. The kiss was long and lavish and so carnal and hungry that Leah felt as if she was being devoured. She couldn't help her wild response, or that she trembled when his big hand closed warmly on her breast. When his lips moved off hers, she still had enough presence of mind to stifle her moan of disappointment. They were clinging to each other almost painfully tight.

His mouth pressed fiercely into her hair before his hot breath gusted into her ear.

"Tell me no, Leah," he rasped. "Do it now, baby."

Leah opened her mouth to speak, then couldn't. Terror, desire, and the unmet needs of a lifetime had just coalesced and focused themselves exclusively on this one man, the man she'd loved for years. Lingering worries about the future seemed to stand at a distance, and she was so unutterably weary of carrying them that all she could feel was relief.

The craving she'd had to love Reece openly and to be loved by him seemed so close now that she could almost reach out and touch them. At least the first part of them, because being loved by Reece—really loved—still seemed as impossible as ever.

And there'd been no declarations of love from either of them. It was too soon for those too. Would they ever come?

"Tell me no, Leah," he repeated hoarsely.

The sudden thought—that there was a time limit on all this in spite of Reece's declaration about their marriage being for life—sent sharp anxiety through her. So many of the good things that had come her way seemed to have time limits. Quick ones.

So many other good things, the biggest ones, were meant to last a lifetime. Parenthood and marriage were the main ones. And yet her parents hadn't wanted the responsibility of raising her or of keeping in contact with her.

Marriages, even some good, seemingly stable ones, ended with alarming frequency. Reece's own good marriage to Rachel had been tragically cut short. Life itself was so easily cut short.

The primal need for more, for everything she might be able to get and everything she was driven to somehow make up for, made it impossible to tell Reece no. The sense that these special days with Reece couldn't last was strong and increased her need.

Not even the terror of being vulnerable to him in the most intimate way possible, was strong enough suddenly to save her from herself. If it all ended tomorrow, next week, next month, or somehow lasted as long as a year, she wanted at least this much. Reece pressed a warm, rough kiss on her shoulder and she felt the prickle of tears.

She turned her face to kiss the side of his neck. His skin was so amazingly smooth there. She couldn't seem to help that her hands moved restlessly on him. He lifted his head from her shoulder only enough to grind out her name.

''Leah?''

It was a last chance she didn't heed, and she was too far gone to answer with anything but an urgently whispered, ''Love me, Reece. Please.''

Little more punctured the thundering silence that followed than the sound of callused hands on soft fabric, the whisper of bodies on fine percale, and their jagged breaths and quiet sighs. The excruciating magic of touch was given and received.

A nightgown was smoothed away, rich sable hair was tangled and stroked. Silky skin was tenderly chafed by hair-rough flesh. Small hands moved with growing confidence as instinct took over and her body learned what gave him pleasure.

And when the many fevered kisses and expert touches brought them together in the deepest and most elemental way, they soared to some lofty, breathless place, a place of sparkling light and sweetness that was nearly unbearable. They hovered there a precious scattering of heartbeats and then began the rippling descent that took them back to earth and landed them softly in the quiet, dimly lit hush of the big bedroom.

They lingered over a last, lazy kiss then lay together skin to skin, overcome by a satisfying lethargy. Leah fell instantly and deeply asleep, so immune to second thoughts and regret that she forgot she'd ever felt such things.

Reece awakened in the night and realized neither of them had turned off the lamp. He didn't bother with it now either.

He'd all but wrapped Leah's small body in his, and he eased back a bit to watch her sleep. Her cheeks were flushed and her beautiful hair was everywhere. He took a lock of it between his thumb and forefinger and rolled it gently, savoring the silky feel of it.

He'd gone too fast with her, and it made him feel like a selfish brute. But the feel of her small body felt good against his. Right. And he wanted her again, though he could wait this time.

It shocked him a little to realize that his desire for Leah last night had banished any thought of Rachel from his mind. Until now. A mental search for Rachel's red-haired, green-eyed image brought nothing. A cold feeling of loss went through him and he felt it collect in his chest.

And yet the crushing sorrow he expected next didn't come. There was no sense of guilt or disloyalty. Instead, his brain conjured the memory of Leah's beautiful eyes going heavy-lidded with pleasure. The sound of her soft breathing made him remember the other night when she'd spoken soothingly to a fussy and overtired little boy. He'd heard her do that before, but it had never affected him like it had that night.

Leah's natural gentleness and sweetness of soul warmed him and gave him solace. The moment he felt it he sensed something deep inside him shift. Just that quickly he knew his grief for Rachel had tucked itself away somewhere, and he felt the coldness in his chest recede.

Leah stirred then, and though she was still deeply asleep, she frowned and made a restless move. He relaxed his hold on her and waited as she rolled over away from him. She'd flung her arm across what was left of her side of the bed and her wrist and hand dangled limply off the edge of the mattress.

Reece smiled at the lovely sight of her soft nudity. If she'd been awake to know she'd shown him so much at once, she'd be head to toe with a fiery blush. He liked that his wife had been untouched until last night. It humbled him to remember that he was the only man she'd ever been with, and to know that every attitude she'd ever have about lovemaking had gotten its start last night with him.

It suddenly mattered very much that he'd treated her with utmost care despite the overwhelming need to have her. It might have been too soon, but he didn't completely regret that. He knew instinctively that Leah could never easily walk away from him now, not when she'd responded to him with such a helpless lack of reserve. And a woman like Leah wouldn't have allowed last night to happen at all unless she'd had her own hope for their marriage to be permanent.

Love me, Reece. Please.

Had she said it that way because she'd meant to use the word love, or because she was more comfortable referring to sex as lovemaking? Leah had probably never spoken a crude or harsh word in her life, so she might automatically choose the word love over sex. She'd no doubt prefer that what they'd done had been love rather than merely sex.

And although she'd been on guard with him for as long as he could remember, she hadn't been on guard when she'd said that.

A settled feeling spread through him and urged him close to her back. He slid his arm across her waist and lifted his head to press a lingering kiss on her bare shoulder. He lowered his cheek to her pillow and closed his eyes. He must have fallen deeply asleep because he didn't know it when Leah managed to slip from beneath his arm long before the alarm clock went off.

They'd forgotten to have the second serving of corn cake last night, and Leah had completely forgotten to tell Reece that Maggie was available to watch Bobby that morning so they could go riding together.

She'd managed to get out of bed without waking Reece and taken a quick shower before she'd gotten dressed. Her hands were trembling as she braided her hair. If she wore it like she normally did, her old Stetson might not fit, and her hair was too long to wear loose while they were riding.

Leah fretted with her hair, then took more pains than usual making sure the light makeup she'd put on was just so. When she finished and tucked in the tail of the long-sleeved blue blouse she'd chosen for that morning, she managed to make a twisted mess of it and had to start over.

No number of other trivial thoughts or obsessive little tasks could truly calm her. She'd been trying not to dwell on how worried she was about facing Reece this morning, but she'd failed miserably. She finally went still and gripped the edge of the bathroom counter before she looked up to closely study herself in the big mirror over the sink.

No one in the world had ever seen her behave as she had with Reece last night. Most people would never have suspected she was capable of that kind of wildness. She hadn't come close to imagining it of herself. Even now, she searched her face for a hint of what might remain, though she couldn't see anything. She closed her eyes and remembered the feeling of it, the almost shameless aggression, the complete lack of self-control.

Whatever secrets she'd thought intimacy might uncover, she'd never expected to have every careful bit of her reserve and self-control stripped away to reveal things even she'd not suspected she was capable of. And she'd never imagined how very vulnerable it was possible to be until Reece had demonstrated it to her. Thoroughly.

What would he think of her this morning?

It was a fact that he'd not seemed to have a single complaint last night. On the other hand, he'd lived without sex for many months, so she doubted he'd have too many complaints about the sudden end of his celibacy.

But it was true that many men lost interest in a woman once they'd had sex. And a woman who allowed sex too soon and too easily was often not taken seriously.

Nearly everything they'd done in this marriage had been out of the natural order. Now they'd had sex before they'd truly developed the nonsexual part of a good relationship. Her reasons for grabbing for every bit of closeness she could have with Reece last night now seemed the height of foolishness. She'd probably doomed the tiny chance she'd had to make this marriage work.

And she'd been such a novice. It was completely possible that he'd been far less carried away by it all than she had.

The moment her mind moved on from that torture to the worry over birth control—in their case, the lack of it—Leah decided she couldn't stand another second of worry and suspense.

Reece was just pulling on his second boot when she stepped out of the bathroom. The moment he glanced at her, his dark gaze warmed and she felt herself relax the tiniest bit. He straightened and walked right to her.

"I take it Maggie can watch the baby this morning," he said as he gripped her waist and bent to give her a gentle kiss.

Her heart quivered with joy at the welcome, and her hands automatically came up to his chest. She felt foolish for being so worried.

"How did you know?"

"You braided your hair. I've seen you do that on the days you take care of the flowers because you always wear a hat. Since those flowers can't possibly need another second of attention this week, I figure you're going riding with me." He smiled. "At least I hope you are."

Reece slid his arms around her as if it was the most natural thing in the world. Leah pushed her hands up his chest and rested them on his wide hard shoulders.

"I didn't know you paid attention to things like that," she said quietly.

"I've been paying attention the last few weeks...but I've been memorizing things the past few days."

He leaned down to kiss her again and his hands moved low to pull her snugly against him. The kiss went carnal then and Leah felt the wildness come crashing back. It took so much to temper her response, but she'd tormented herself with enough worry about it that it was important to demonstrate, at least to herself, that she had some self-control. Even then, she found herself beginning to slip over the line.

The pressure of Reece's mouth eased away just enough for him to growl against her lips, "Oh, darlin', how 'bout I just have you for breakfast?"

It was hard to cling to at least a bit of common sense. When his lips skimmed across her jaw to lightly nibble her neck just below her ear, she could barely form a coherent thought.

"M-Maggie said she could be here at six," she managed to get out.

It felt so, so wonderful to be pressed up against his hard masculine body and remember what it had felt like last night skin to skin. When his warm breath feathered over her ear she gasped raggedly at the stark pleasure it caused.

"I think we need a honeymoon someplace," he rasped. "No work, no people, nothing but the two of us."

"What about...Bobby?" she said breathlessly, staggered by the touch of his tongue on a sensitive spot even as her heart leaped with joy at Reece's suggestion and what it meant.

As if on cue, they both heard a happy, good-natured "Mommee" from the partially opened door to the next room.

Reece's low chuckle sounded strained. "We've got an early bird."

He gave her a lingering kiss on the cheek then resolutely eased away a space. His dark gaze was heavy-lidded. Leah let her hands slide down his chest and she eased back a little more. He caught her fingers and gripped them a few seconds before they heard Bobby call out again, impatiently this time.

"Mommeeee."

"Maybe you could see to the boy, Mommy. I'd better shave." He leaned down for a swift, hard kiss then released her hands, though he seemed reluctant to do so. When he did, Leah moved away from him to the connecting door on legs that still felt deliciously weak.

But she could have danced on air! She'd never imagined a man could look at her the way Reece just had. *As if he loved her.*

Excitement, expectation and happiness whirled so strongly inside her that she felt like she was floating as she got Bobby dressed for the day. Reece joined her in time to carry the child as they went to the kitchen.

By the time they finished breakfast and the dishes were cleared away, Maggie arrived. Bobby didn't protest being left behind because Maggie had brought along an oversize inflatable ball that he'd immediately wanted to play with.

The early morning was already warm but perfect. Reece chose a pretty black mare for her and took his big sorrel. They planned to ride to one of the creeks not far from the headquarters. It was to be a relaxed ride, and not as long as it could have been since Leah wasn't used to riding.

"Don't want to cripple you up," Reece declared after he explained what he had in mind. She agreed but had insisted on saddling the horse herself, though it had been so long since she'd done it that she was slow. Reece waited while she worked and he'd shown no sign of impatience, though he checked to make sure the cinch was tight enough when she finished. To her consternation, he'd taken up a good six inches of slack in the cinch strap with one expert pull before he secured the excess and let down the stirrup.

Once they were mounted and riding down one of the alleys that cut through the network of corrals, Leah glanced his way.

"Have you decided about going to Hoyt's tomorrow?"

Reece sent her a sparkling glance. "It'll be my pleasure to take you, Leah. I apologize for making you wonder."

Leah smiled. It was as if she'd stepped into an alternative universe that morning. One so beautiful and perfect that it was suddenly everything she'd dreamed of.

They were on their way back to the house from the creek before the perfection began to worry her. The first dark tendrils of guilt began their insidious rise. The worst of that concerned Rachel, but she couldn't let herself face that one yet. The guilt that seemed most immediate—and most in need of confessing—was about birth control.

It was something they should have discussed, something she should have thought about long before last night. But when you were married to a man who never touched you, being on the pill wasn't necessary. And the notion of becoming pregnant with Reece's child was anything but undesirable. She loved Bobby so much that she'd love to have a little brother or sister for him. At least one of each. Bobby shouldn't grow up an only child as she and Reece had.

Though Reece had once told her he was willing to have other children with her, she needed to know if that was still all right with him. And like so many other things in their marriage, a pregnancy now would be too soon so they'd need to do something about birth control. She waited until he glanced her way then made a nervous start.

"You told me months ago that you didn't object to having other children with me," she said, then added, "Has that changed?" She couldn't help that she held her breath as she waited for what he would say.

A gleam of humor sparkled in his dark eyes. "Did we make a baby last night?"

Leah relaxed and shook her head.

"The time wasn't right, but we'll need to use something until I can get a prescription."

Reece's rugged face went somber. "You'll marry me, won't you, if I wind up pregnant?"

The outrageous question startled a giggle out of her. Reece grinned. "I don't mind living dangerously, Leah, but you're the one who has carry for nine months. You decide when."

He reached over and caught her hand to give it a squeeze. "So yes, I do want more kids." His fingers tightened.

His horse crowded against the mare and he tugged her closer as he leaned toward her for a quick kiss. His lips touched hers and sent a bolt of feeling through her, but then a massive wave of emotion surged up. As Reece pulled away and released her hand, that massive wave was still strong enough to make her eyes smart.

She truly had stepped into a beautiful alternative universe that morning. The relief and gratitude and joy of it all was almost unbearable.

And yet neither of them had spoken love words. Though she'd couldn't have done the things she'd done for Reece and with him without being deeply in love with him, she knew very well that Reece might be able to do and say everything he had without being "in love" with her. He could out of gratitude and friendship and certainly affection, but unless he told her what his exact feelings were, she had no real way to be certain.

Then again, perhaps she needed to let the whole notion go. Reece was showing her in so many ways that she mattered to him, that he cared about her. When she thought about how grateful she was to finally have the man she loved care about her and respond to her, she realized she'd gotten greedy.

Reece was bending over backward to demonstrate his desire to stay married to her. Why should she expect him to jump through one more hoop?

Just a handful of days ago things had been so lifeless between them that the only chance of happiness for either of them had seemed to be divorce. Since then, the earth had not only shifted on its axis, it had reversed the poles. Night had exchanged places with day, and the chill of near-estrangement had been banished by the balmy temperature of mutual desire and companionship.

Besides, Reece still loved Rachel. She couldn't expect him to simply switch off a love that had been that deep and powerful, or to suddenly decide he was in love with someone else. After all, she'd never been able to stop loving him, not even when he'd married Rachel.

What she did believe was that he'd made a little space in his heart that was completely hers. As long as she remembered that and allowed herself to be content, she could live without extravagant declarations.

But how long would she be able to keep from making an extravagant declaration of her own?

CHAPTER TEN

ONCE they returned to the house and Maggie had gone home, Reece was so doggedly determined to get the rings that he whisked her away to San Antonio. Marie had been able to keep Bobby in town, so they were able to take the trip by themselves.

Leah only barely thwarted Reece's enthusiasm for buying the most spectacular—and no doubt, the most expensive—rings they found. She neatly distracted him by insisting on a wedding ring for him.

"I don't wear rings," he'd said gruffly, and she'd had to insist.

His next try, "I'd lose a finger out working," brought her quick, "You could put it in your pocket."

He'd finally agreed and tried on a few handsome choices when Leah remembered that Rachel had never been able to persuade him to wear a wedding ring. The fact that he was indulging Leah now was a pleasant surprise.

In the meantime, she found the perfect rings. They were beautiful and elegant, but not as flashy as Rachel's had been. The only real disagreement between them happened when it came time to pay and Leah insisted on paying for Reece's ring.

She'd always lived frugally and still had savings, though the ring would put a hefty dent in them. Her reminder that this was a ring exchange ended his protest.

They had lunch at a wonderful San Antonio restaurant, then started home. Bobby had finished his nap and was ready to go by the time they got to Marie's to pick him up.

Leah's heart was full, and the quiet joy she felt was easily the best of her life. Each moment they spent together was profoundly sweet, and she reveled in their growing closeness. The sense that they were truly connected made her feel relaxed and optimistic, and that she could confide anything to him.

The craving to tell Reece how much she loved him was so intense that it took everything she had not to do it. Only the fact that she could never be the one to say it first deterred her, though it was already hard to guard her words.

Ironically, it was thinking about how hard it would be to keep from telling Reece she loved him that brought her guilt about Rachel roaring up.

In view of how much she loved Reece and her complete loss of control and common sense last night, she suddenly had real worries about what she might say in the heat of the moment.

A simple, "I love you," might easily come out as a helplessly candid, "I've loved you so long." And now that Reece seemed to miss nothing, it would be natural for him to wonder—or to even ask— how long that had been.

She'd been in love with Reece since the summer before her senior year of high school. The foster parents she'd lived with back then used to own a small ranch in the area, so she'd seen Reece often enough.

He'd been seven years older than she, and he'd taken charge of Waverly interests after his father's death the year before. She'd been nothing but a teenage kid to him, but he'd always taken time to say something kind to the homely nobody most people overlooked.

Perpetually starved for attention, Leah had been completely smitten, though she'd only confessed that to Rachel one time in the beginning. Leery of being teased, she'd not mentioned it again. She'd tried very hard to appear aloof to Reece, though she'd lived for even a glimpse of him.

Leah and Rachel had been twenty when Reece had started dating Rachel, and their instant love affair became a sudden marriage that had devastated Leah. Somehow she'd made peace with that.

After all, it wasn't as if Reece would ever fall for her, much less marry her. She'd chosen to be glad that the two people she loved most were in love with each other, though she'd never been able to stop her feelings for Reece. She'd felt tremendous guilt for that because she'd seen it as a betrayal of her best friend.

Though she doubted her feelings fit into the traditional definition of adultery, her conscience had been so tender about it that it might as well have been the primary one.

Particularly after Rachel had died, and Leah had jumped at the chance to marry Reece when he'd asked. The weight of that knowledge, and the guilt she still felt for taking advantage of him at a vulnerable time, suddenly made her deeply uneasy.

Should she confess it all to Reece or not? The question nagged at her the rest of the afternoon and evening.

That night, she was so quickly and completely swept away by Reece's lovemaking that she forgot all about her guilt and her worries about love words slipping out.

The sleeveless sundress Leah had bought for the barbecue had a fitted bodice with a deep V and a gathered waistline that flared to a full skirt. The bright red, orange, gold and blue vertical stripes flattered her and looked festive.

While Bobby played nearby late Saturday afternoon, Leah surveyed herself in the full length mirror in the master bed-room, smoothing the bodice into place.

Reece walked into the closet behind her and she glanced toward his reflection. He'd chosen to wear a pair of dark blue jeans and his usual white shirt, but this one featured scrolling white embroidery on the Western-cut yoke that gave the shirt a faint glow, and emphasized his weathered tan. The glowing white and dark blue next to her colorful dress was complimentary, and the contrasts made them stand out.

Reece slid his hands around her waist from behind and nuzzled the side of her neck. He'd folded back the long sleeves of his shirt as he normally did, and she lifted her hands to rest them on his bare wrists, loving the hard feel of his hair-roughened skin and the thick muscles beneath.

"You look beautiful, Leah," he breathed, then glanced into the mirror to make eye contact with her reflection. "It's gonna be hard to share you with a crowd tonight.''

The sexy look in his eyes was a promise for later, and she felt her body react.

''By the way, the baby-sitter's here,'' he said, then pressed his lips against her hair. A tingling weakness went through her and she felt herself melt. Since she was watching in the mirror she saw the way he closed his eyes on the kiss, as if he was savoring it.

''Did you show her the list I made?'' she asked a little breathlessly. She'd made a list of emergency numbers, including Reece's cell phone and the number for Donovan ranch, along with a list of where to find things for Bobby. She'd also prepared a casserole the sitter could pop in the oven, and she'd made certain there were selections of soft drinks and snacks.

''Not yet. We probably ought to show her around the house.''

He loosened his arms and Leah stepped away to get her handbag. Reece picked up Bobby and they all went out to show Marie's sister Melody around, then Leah waited while the teenager read through the list she'd made in case she had questions.

Bobby protested briefly when they kissed him goodbye, but he was acquainted with Melody from his visits to Marie's day care, so the girl easily calmed him.

Once they were on the highway for the fairly short drive to Donovan ranch, there were no distractions from Leah's feelings of guilt. Although nothing she'd done that day had helped her to truly escape them, they seemed to grow worse with each mile they traveled. By the time they arrived at the Donovan Ranch and Reece parked the SUV under a tree in the front yard, she realized worry was tainting everything.

It was becoming increasingly clear that her conscience wouldn't let up. The part of her that remembered in excruciating detail how it had felt to be rejected and abandoned by her mother and father, was terrified that history would repeat itself with Reece.

Though she'd not deserved what had happened to her as a child, her disloyalty to Rachel and her eagerness to take advantage of Reece's marriage proposal were certainly worthy of comeuppance.

And yet there was another part of her that assured her it was safe to confide in Reece. The man who'd been sensitive enough to be kind to a lonely teenager would surely understand.

What he wouldn't understand was her betrayal of her best friend and the fact that she'd essentially taken advantage of him at a vulnerable time. After all, she could have tried to reason with him about his worries and perhaps helped him find a solution for protecting Bobby that wasn't as drastic as marrying her. But she'd kept silent, hardly daring to believe her good luck.

Until the day they'd stood in front of the judge and she began to realize exactly what it was that she'd been about to do. And by then it had been too late.

Hoyt had seen them drive in and met them on the lawn.

"Too bad you brought the killjoy, darlin'," he said as he took her hand and gave it a squeeze.

Leah couldn't help her startled laugh. Reece reached over to gently remove Leah's hand from Hoyt's and give him a reproving look.

"Where's Eadie hidin' out?"

Hoyt's grin fell a bit. "Eadie's hidin' out where she always does. At home."

"Probably tired of handling your social calendar. Which new Saturday night gal did you invite? The blonde with the ratty hair or the brunette who can't figure out how to button her blouses?'' Reece aimed a sparkling glance at Leah who only barely managed not to laugh at the apt description of the women Hoyt usually dated. ''Pardon the blunt talk, darlin'.''

''I didn't invite either of them,'' Hoyt grumbled. ''I asked Eadie to come over, even told her she didn't have to dress up if she didn't want to. I offered to teach her to dance—again—but she said she's not interested in dancing.''

''She's not interested in men,'' Reece commented.

Hoyt's expression went a little grim. ''Reckon not.''

His obvious disappointment over Eadie's absence made Leah curious. It almost sounded as if he had feelings for Eadie, which was surprising since Eadie was nothing like the glamorous beauties Hoyt usually dated.

Leah actually knew very little about Eadie Webb, since she'd been a couple years ahead of Leah in school. And Eadie didn't socialize much at all.

The three of them walked to the huge, heavily shaded backyard and mixed with the crowd. The food tables were crammed with various hot weather dishes and Hoyt left them to help take up the last of the beef and carry the large platters of meat to the tables. After everyone started through the buffet lines, they filled their plates and the three of them sat together at one of the tables.

The food was excellent, and the crowd virtually picked the buffet tables clean. The desserts on the dessert table went next. As the early evening air began to cool, the country band began to tune up. Hoyt had had the wooden dance floor set up on the section of lawn that was most protected from the evening sun.

He managed to persuade Reece to let him have the first dance with Leah, but only because Reece made him forfeit the other two dances he'd planned with her. The first dance was a rollicking one, and Leah was laughing by the time the number ended and Hoyt passed her into Reece's arms.

Reece was also a fine dancer, and patient enough to give her a few lessons at the edge of the dance floor. Later, when some of the couples started dancing the Cotton-Eyed Joe, Reece coaxed her to give it a whirl and they took their place in the large circle. By the time the music stopped, Leah had managed to get at least a small part of the dance right.

They sat out the next few dances to visit with other guests, before Reece led her to the dance floor for a couple of the ballads.

"Looks like Hoyt's finally given up on Eadie," Reece remarked to her during the second dance. Leah glanced in Hoyt's direction to see him leaning against a tree trunk, solemnly watching the dancers.

"I didn't know Hoyt was interested in her."

"He's not, he only thinks he is. She's one of the rare unmarried females he's ever been around who doesn't fall all over herself to get his attention, so she's the rare unmarried female he takes seriously."

Reece grinned down at her. "Might be a case of wanting what he knows he can't have. The fact that Eadie doesn't date and doesn't seem interested in men—him in particular—just adds to the fascination."

Leah had never dated either, mostly because she'd never been asked. She'd refused Rachel's matchmaking schemes, and she'd stayed home or done things with friends when she wasn't working. The fact that Eadie didn't try to get Hoyt's attention was also telling, and she suspected Eadie's no-show was far more significant than either Reece or Hoyt had guessed.

It was the perfect description of Leah's life, both before and after Reece had married Rachel. Leah, of all people, knew what it was like to secretly be in love with someone you were certain would never love you. She'd gone out of her way to hide her feelings, particularly after Reece and Rachel had started dating.

In Hoyt's case, he was something of a womanizer, which would probably make Eadie doubly wary of taking any sign of interest from him seriously. And she probably thought he'd only invited her tonight to be polite. There was nothing worse than a token invitation. If Eadie had feelings for Hoyt that she thought were hopeless, she'd avoid being around him, particularly at a social event at his home.

The whole issue of one-sided, secret feelings, whether they were Hoyt's or Eadie's, suddenly brought back the guilt she'd been able to set aside the past couple of hours. She didn't realize her upset had shown until Reece's low voice penetrated her worried thoughts.

"Something wrong?"

Leah glanced up hesitantly, then away. It was probably the most perfect opening she'd ever have, but the risk she was taking was so monumental that she wasn't sure she had the courage. And the dance was no place for confessions.

"I'd...like to talk about it. Later," she said, then glanced up at him again. His rugged face went a little somber and she could tell by the way he searched her face that she'd passed the point of no return. She had to tell him now.

It was nearing eleven by the time they'd had their fill of dancing. Leah had promised Melody's mother that they'd make sure the teenager had time to get home by midnight, so they needed to leave.

After they made their way along the edge of the crowd, saying goodnight to neighbors and friends, they found Hoyt and thanked him for the fine evening. The ride home was increasingly tense, and neither of them spoke.

Melody reported that Bobby had needed to be rocked to sleep, but that the evening went well. Reece saw her off. Leah took a few moments to call Melody's mother to let her know the girl had just started the drive back to town.

Reece had walked through the house turning off lights, so he was waiting when she hung up the phone in the kitchen.

She turned toward him. "Would you like something to drink?"

"Nothing for me, thanks," he said, his low voice quiet. "What was it you wanted to talk about?"

Leah was too restless to sit down. She felt awkward and edgy, and gripped her hands in front of her waist while she fumbled for a start.

"I was thinking tonight while you were talking about Hoyt, that maybe it was Eadie who might...have feelings for him."

Her theory seemed to amuse him and he smiled. "Honey, if she's got feelings for Hoyt, she's got a funny way of showing it."

Leah tried to force herself to smile, but it probably looked as flat as it felt. "She might not, but thinking about it made me realize that I needed to tell you about something I did. Something very wrong. More than one thing, actually, and you need to know."

Reece gave her a skeptical look. "What could you have done that was so bad?"

She took a breath, but was too tense to get in much air. And then she wasn't sure how to make a start. Her heart was suddenly pounding and she felt her eyes sting.

"I had feelings for a married man," she said quietly, and felt the sting intensify at her cowardly wording.

"I never did anything about those feelings," she went on, "not a single thing. And no one knew, not even Rachel. Until now."

Reece moved closer and she stared at his chest, willing herself not to cry or lose her nerve.

"Are you still in love with him?" She could tell by the grim tone in Reece's voice that he was suddenly taking this seriously.

"I was seventeen when I first met him." She glanced up at him briefly but couldn't make eye contact before her gaze dropped. "I had a terrible crush on him. He was handsome and gallant, and I'm absolutely certain he never suspected."

It took her a moment to regain control of the emotion that was roaring higher. There was no sense keeping either of them in suspense, so she took another shallow breath that didn't feel like nearly enough.

"And when he fell in love with my best friend then later married her, I couldn't seem to stop loving him."

She felt Reece's surprise and turned to walk a few shaky steps away. She pressed a fist against her lips, her heart pounding sickly in the silence. She eased her fist away to go on.

"Loving you was disloyal to Rachel and a betrayal of her friendship." The words tumbled out then, along with the tears he couldn't see. "I took advantage of you at a vulnerable time. Over these past few weeks I realized I couldn't stand for you to go on being unhappy, so I offered you the divorce. I thought it might make up for the wrong of everything else."

It was so hard to keep her voice steady. "But then everything happened so quick this week. I started thinking we might have a chance to be happy and you'd never have to know."

Now that she'd got most of it out, she felt some of the pressure ebb slightly. "But I know. And now, you know too."

The tears that had been streaking silently down her cheeks were blinding now, and she tried to wipe them away with her hands as she waited for Reece to react. She couldn't hear anything over the loud roar of blood in her ears.

When Reece's big hands settled warmly on her waist, she flinched a little. And then his arms slid around her and tightened as he bent to press his lean cheek against hers.

"Oh, darlin'," he rasped, "darlin'."

Leah's felt her heart quiver at his tender tone. He kissed her cheek then pressed his jaw even tighter against hers. "I never, never guessed, but it was me who took advantage. You loved Bobby and I used your devotion to get what I wanted. I deprived you of a husband who'd love only you, and it didn't help any more to remind myself that I'd married you to protect the boy. But then you walked into the den the other night and dropped that little bombshell."

He lifted his head and loosened his hold. Leah's fist was still pressed against her lip. She was stiff, balanced on the razor edge of dread.

I deprived you of a husband who'd love only you. It sounded like a confirmation that Rachel would always have the lion's share of his heart.

She didn't resist when he turned her toward him. He gently pulled her hand down and she looked up into his eyes. Her voice was hoarse. "The worst is that I betra—"

Reece's finger came up to her lips to gently silence her. "You never said a single word, you never gave me so much as a look, Leah, whatever it was you felt." He gave her a faint smile. "Fact is, I thought for the longest time you didn't like me at all."

Leah felt the first trickle of real relief, and she went weak with it as her tension began to ease away.

"I tried so hard to stop caring for you," she said shakily. "So very hard."

"Caring about someone, loving them, isn't something you can turn on and off like a faucet," he said gruffly. "It's either there or it isn't. You act on it or you don't. You didn't act, you didn't do a single thing to hurt or hinder Rachel's marriage to me. I reckon that proves you were more loyal to Rachel and her happiness than to whatever it was you felt for me."

He paused and a faint smile eased across his mouth. "As far as you taking advantage of me in a weak moment, I reckon we're even. And the way it's working out, it looks like getting married was something we would have come to in time anyway. You still would have been coming around to see Bobby, and I was bound to look at you like I did the other day and finally see you. One way or the other, we woulda ended up in this kitchen some night."

He lifted his hands to her damp cheeks to tenderly cradle her face. She lifted her hands to his lean waist.

"So I damned sure hope you still love me, Mrs. Waverly," he growled, "because I'm in love with you now."

Elation shot through her, and Reece's lips settled on hers for a long, sweetly gentle kiss.

He eased away only far enough away to whisper, "Never figured to ever feel like this again, like I'm whole.'' He pulled her into his arms to tightly hold her. "You did that for me, Leah. I love you, baby."

Her heart went wild with happiness, and she held on to Reece for dear life. "I love you so much," she got out, "always. Always."

Reece loosened his arms and bent to pick her up, taking a moment to kiss her again before he started across the big kitchen. He switched off the kitchen light with his elbow, then strode through the dark house to the hall and the bedrooms.

They made a brief detour through Bobby's room to look in on him, then Reece carried her on into their room. He nudged the connecting door almost closed then carried her to the bed.

Their lovemaking that night was both a sweet celebration and the glorious prelude to a long, contented life together. There were other children. Three more. The girls came next, but Bobby had to wait for a kid brother.

The memory of a lost lover and best friend was kept fondly close, but the hurt of the past mellowed to a dimly felt, bittersweet ache, soothed away by a love and tender devotion that regularly lit their contented hearts with bursts of glittering joy.